"The Empty Beach"

The Soundtrack To My Life trilogy

Book one

Jody Clark

DEDICATION

For all my family & friends, especially Erica and Owen for their endless support and encouragement!

ACKNOWLEDGMENTS

Thanks to Fairlee Anderson for the cover design.
Thanks to Corey Cain Photography for the cover postcard photo.

The characters, dialogue, and scenes are loosely based on real people and events, but make no doubt about it – this book is a work of fiction!

I'm sure there were many times I probably took my summers at York Beach for granted, but looking back on it now, I am so very fortunate to have grown up in such a beautiful place!

For Tony, Jason, Tim, Ian, and all the 'summer friends' who have come in & out of my life over the years. No matter how long or short the friendships – you've all left a handprint on my life!

Jody Clark

1

"STORY OF MY LIFE" - Social Distortion

I suppose like most people, music has always been a huge influence on my life, on my moods, and certainly on my attempt at finding love. In my first two years of high school, my musical taste was pretty much relegated to top 40 music. The Police, Prince, Huey Lewis, or whatever else mainstream radio or MTV put out there. Truth be told, I was a huge Howard Jones fan. Most of you, especially in the iGeneration will have to google that shit, but trust me, not only was he a brilliant keyboardist, but he was 'positive pop' personified.

It wasn't until my junior year that my musical taste morphed into a bit more darker realms; realms which included Depeche Mode, The Smiths, The Jesus and Mary

Chain, New Order, and of course, The Cure. Ironically, I didn't get into this type of music because I was sad or depressed (that would come later), I got into it because the girl who I had a crush on was totally into them. Cara Montgomery. And what better way to get into a girl's heart than to get into her music, right? Notice I said 'get into her heart', NOT into her pants. Although, in high school, and I suppose in life, those lines get blurred sometimes. But in this case, I was sincerely just trying to get into her heart. Anyway, my crush was crushed, and my feelings were returned as unrequited.

Ironically, these bands that I only started listening to because of her, began to take on a whole new light to me. Albeit a darker light, but one that I would slowly fall in love with. Up until that point, I only thought bands like Reo Speedwagon, Air Supply, or Chicago could put love lost into perspective. I was wrong. These new bands on my playlist, especially The Cure, seemed to capture my feelings more concisely. They were sadder, yet more relatable.

So just like that, I went from being inspired by the positive vibes of Howard Jones' "Things Can Only Get Better," to getting depressed to songs like "Unloveable" by The Smiths.

My goal was to narrow this trilogy down to three different summers of my life; three summers that made the biggest impact on me. Even though the summers of '87 & '88 were key to forming the musical foundation of my future, I decided not to choose either of them for this book.

Also, keep in mind, the 'biggest impact' is different from most fun. If this was based on that, I would have easily picked the summer of '89 to be my focus on this book. But despite being wild, fun, and crazy, I felt it didn't really have an actual storyline. It was just a bunch of random, silly scenes. A collage of craziness, if you will.

The summer of '89 was also one of the few summers that I didn't have any significant crushes on anyone. Maybe that was part of the reason it was so fun.

Some of my fondest memories of my friends were from 1989; the parties, the lazy beach days, shooting hoops, and our late-night walkabouts. Not to mention, my flirting game had significantly improved. There were three important and memorable things that happened to me that summer.

1) Sex. Like real sex. With someone other than myself. I know, I know, I was a late bloomer. It was with Staci Belanger. She was here on vacation with her friend Taylor Collins. The first time we met was at the Aqua Lounge (under twenty-one night). I was hanging with one of my best friends that night, Scott, and I remember spending most of the night on the dance floor trying to show off for the girls.

It was hard to tell which dance moves won them over. Was it to "It Takes Two" by Rob Base? Or was it our sweet hip hop moves to Kool Moe Dee's "Wild, Wild West"? Personally, I think the girls liked it when we *Push*ed it, *Push*ed it real good.

Either way, we all left together soon after the classic Aqua Lounge anthem was played. You know, the anthem that stated the roof was on fire and that we should forego using water and to let the mother fucker burn.

We ended up walking the beach with the girls, and it was a little later that night that I became a man! Well, it really wasn't that dramatic or life-changing, but it was a fuckin' good time! So much so, that Staci and I "hung" out multiple times that week.

2) The second coolest thing that summer was when "Say Anything" with John Cusack came out. Not only did I love it, but I related so well to the Lloyd Dobler character. Still to this day, that movie remains a solid top three on my list.

I was so inspired by the movie and John Cusack that I wanted to write my own movie and have him star in it...like right here in Maine. No, seriously, I did.

What kind of writing experience did I have? Besides some cheesy love letters and some cheesier poems, I had no experience. None. Zero. I had taken a creative writing class my junior year in high school which I got a solid C in, but other than that, I had never taken any real classes on writing; certainly none that taught you the art of screenwriting. But how hard could it be? I had an amazing story in my head. Sorta.

I was going to draw on my *vast* nineteen year life-experiences and crank out a script for John Cusack to star in. I'd base the characters on my friends and on real conversations we had, and of course I'd base John Cusack's character after myself. I started thinking of all the funny stories and conversations we had over the past summers, and I couldn't help but to crack myself up. The movie was practically writing itself.

3) The third big thing that happened in '89 was the release of The Cure's epic record, "Disintegration". It was dark, moody, and full of sadness and regret. In other words, I fuckin' loved it!

I just remember reading the lyrics and thinking how beautifully sad and well-written they were. Like I said in the beginning, music, especially introspective music, has always played a huge part in shaping my life, and the "Disintegration" album is at the top of that list. '89 was also the first of many times I'd see them live in concert.

Oh, let me jump back to #2 for a second; the whole *John Cusack- Say Anything- I'm gonna write a movie* thing. It wasn't until the fall of '89, but I did sit down and 'attempt' to write my screenplay.

I was living in the next town over (Kittery) with a high school friend, Alex. Kittery is Maine's southernmost town. Also, Fun Fact: Kittery is Maine's oldest town.

Anyway, Alex was gone for the weekend so I thought it would be the perfect time to write my York Beach movie masterpiece. I bought a brand new notebook, a new pen, and I even bought a book called "Writing Screenplays 101". True story.

I spent that summer creating a lot of random scenes, characters, and dialogue. I knew how I wanted to start the screenplay, and I knew how I wanted it to end, and I figured the middle would write itself. So, with the Cure blaring out and with candles lit, I wrote and wrote and wrote. By the time I passed out, I probably had filled twenty or thirty notebook pages.

When I woke up the next morning, I eagerly read what I had written. My eager and excited smile quickly faded into a disheartened frown. It was shit. Utter shit! Absolutely none of what was in my head translated onto the paper...at all! I was tempted to blame the new pen, but I knew better.

I was never the type of person who quit or gave up on things easily. I knew that it took writers many, many, many drafts to perfect their work, but... but this was a totally shitty draft. It was at that point where reality set in. It was also at that point when I started majorly chastising myself.

"You're a fuckin' idiot, Josh! Did you really think it'd be that easy to write a movie? People spend years going to school for this shit and you think you can just buy a *Writing 101* book and have success? And do you really think John Cusack is gonna come to York, Maine to star in your piece of shit movie? Fuck no!! Fuck! Fuck! FUCK!"

In my disappointed angst and haste, I went into the kitchen and grabbed my plastic recycling bin. I threw my notebook (and pen) into it and lit them on fire. It burned quickly, and within minutes, all that was left was a semi-melted pen, ashes, and a burn spot on the bottom of the bin. It would be eleven years before I ever sat down to write anything again. Eleven years.

Anyway, the summer of '89 was super-fun, but it's not where I'm going to start this story. And I'm also not going to use any of my high school summers. I only brought up my high school years to point out it was because of Cara Montgomery that my future mixtape playlists would be filled with the bands she introduced me to. So I'm thinking I'll start this story at age twenty-five. The summer of 1995 to be exact.

My friends used to make fun of me for being the king of the mixtape. It's one thing to make mixes for parties and whatnot, but when you find yourself making mixes for every girl you fall for, I suppose that could be considered a bit much. Maybe I should clarify that. I didn't actually make a mixtape for every girl I had a crush on or liked. Come on, give me some credit. Doing that would definitely be pathetic. I limited my mixes to only the handful (big handful) who had truly touched my heart over the years. That's sweet, right?

My best friend, Doug, has a theory for everything. One of his theories concerning relationships is this: The three things that are a certain kiss of death are

1) Giving a girl flowers.

2) Telling her that you *like* her before she tells you.

3) Making her a mixtape.

Guilty, guilty, and guilty. I hate when his theories are right. Whether making the mixes were sweet, pathetic, or even the kiss of death, it should be noted that all of the songs were carefully chosen by me for that specific girl. And each tape, like each girl, had a deep and specific meaning to me.

Doug also has a theory that only 71% of the girls even listened to the mixtapes I made for them. He has no actual proof to back up his number, but sadly, I have no proof otherwise. I'm sure he's probably right to an extent, but I'd like to think they all listened to them. I suppose, secretly, I hope that years later when they stumble on the old mixtape, that they give it another listen, smile, and remember the moments we shared. Also, if truth be told, I hope that ten years hence, they listen and kick themselves for walking away.

And if the real, real truth is to be told, I sometimes create a scenario in which they show up at my door ten years later with the tape in their hand, a tear of regret in their eye, and a 'I was a fool and I want you back' speech in their hearts. And no, I've never shared those scenarios with Doug. Shhhh.

So, in honor of all these songs which provided a sad yet beautiful soundtrack to my life over the years, I'll be using them as my chapter titles. And before you call me out on it, the song placements don't necessarily have a rhyme or reason behind them. Some fit the chapters perfectly, some don't even coincide with the year the story takes place. That's just how I wanted it done. Deal with it. When you write your own book, you can do it how you want.

2

"DON'T CHANGE" - INXS

(Summer of 1995)

In the summer of '95, I was twenty-five years old and had just moved back to Maine. I was just coming off a nine month relationship with Liz Hannigan. Well, technically it was more like five months but more on that later. Although it was my longest relationship to date, when it ended, I was probably the least devastated I've ever been. The relationship just sort of ran its course. There was no big infidelity or huge fight, the spark just never turned into a flame for either one of us.

I suppose I should tell you where this story takes place, especially considering the setting has as much to do with the story and my life as the music does. I grew up in York, Maine, which is one of the southern-most towns in Maine. York Beach is the quintessential family summer beach town. The beach is mostly comprised of quaint tourist shops, restaurants, and a few bars scattered about. York Beach is also home to a seaside amusement park and zoo (York's Wild Kingdom & Amusement Park). Do NOT think Six Flags, and DO NOT think San Diego Zoo!! It's mostly a little kid park with the Scrambler being the highlight of excitement.

The beach is basically separated into 3 sections – Long Sands, Short Sands, and the Harbor Beach. The Harbor Beach is the smallest but most private area of the three. Long Sands is obviously the longest stretch of beach, yet only has a couple of beachfront stores and restaurants. While Short Sands is a much smaller beach, it is where the majority of all the beach businesses are located.

Short Sands is also home to York's three most iconic beach businesses. The previously mentioned York's Wild Kingdom is one of them. The other is the beachfront arcade Fun-O-Rama. As soon as your feet step onto the wide, creaking wooden floor, you're greeted with all the typical sights and sounds of an arcade. From the classic older games to the newer, more hip ones, the Fun-O-Rama has it all. The side wall is lined with ticket games, including the ever popular Skee-ball.

The centerpiece of the arcade is the Foosball table. Not only were many bets lost there, but the Foosball table was a great place for horny teenage boys to show-off to (not as blatant, but equally horny) girls. I know that all sounds silly and stupid, but many a summer's night hookup stemmed directly from the "Foos". Of course, this was more designated to younger teens (14-16). The seventeen and older girls took A LOT more to impress than just a silly Foosball show-off match.

The final iconic business at the beach is the Goldenrod. In addition to being a full service restaurant, it has an old-fashioned ice cream counter and a large selection of nostalgic penny candies. Equally as large, yet much more expensive, is their selection of home-made fudge. But, by far, the biggest attraction there is the giant taffy machine. It's strategically placed in the front window. At any point throughout the day while the taffy was being hand-made, it would be commonplace for there to be a dozen or so tourists with their faces pressed against the window. Between the oohs and aahs and cameras flashing, you would think they were witnessing the 4th of July fireworks.

Okay, back to the Liz Hannigan story: I first met Liz in July, 1994. She was twenty-three and here on vacation for a week with her family. She loved this place so much that she also returned here for a week in August with a bunch of her friends.

On that particular summer of '94, I was trying out a new job at a local landscaping company. I didn't hate it, but I certainly didn't love it. My friend Pete got me the job, so even on the days it sucked, it was at least good to have a friend to share in the misery.

I met Liz on my day off. My three best friends, Pete, Doug, and Scott had just finished shooting hoops and were having some slices over at Paras Pizza. Liz sat across from us with her parents and her little brother. Two things caught my eye:

1) She was super-sexy. Not sexy-hot, but more like sexy-cute. The four of us friends are totally split on which one is better.

2) She wore a Depeche Mode tee from their tour last year. A tour which I attended. Actually, a third thing caught my eye as well: She had amazing boobs (I'm just keepin' it real here).

Anyway, when she went to get a soda refill, I used that as my moment. I also used her tee-shirt as my conversation starter. She was from Rhode Island, and come to find out, was at the exact same Depeche Mode show as I was last fall.

When she found out I was a resident of York, she provided me with the perfect setup when she asked, *What's there to do around here?* From that point on, I anointed myself her personal tour guide. Seeing as this was their first day in town, she was supposed to spend it doing 'family' things. I mentioned to her that I was a DJ at a club that night and asked if she wanted to go and hang out with me.

We hit it off immediately. Emotionally and physically. Like I said, she had such a fun time that week, she came back later in the summer with some of her friends. Between her friends and my friends, every night was party central. After she left, we stayed in close contact. As in, the type of contact that consisted of long late night phone calls. A couple of times, I even drove down to Rhode Island to see her on my days off.

Sometime in early October, she told me her roommate was moving out and joked that I should move in. By Halloween, the joke turned into reality. Besides my friends and family, there was really nothing tying me to York. Certainly not my job.

Liz's dad owned a few retail stores, and considering that she was the manager, she got me a job. I had never done or desired to do retail before, but I was just excited to be moving in with a girl I liked. A sexy-cute girl.

Unfortunately, our sparkly summer excitement slowly dulled and faded. Don't get me wrong, it never got to the point where we hated each other, and it never even got to the point where we disliked each other. It just became obvious that not all summer romances should be pursued.

I'd like to think I've learned some valuable life lessons from the experience.

1) If anyone out there is considering marriage (not that I was) you should definitely live together first.

2) If your relationship only consists of a sporadic two week fling and some late night calls, DO NOT move in together.

3) If you do live with someone, DO NOT work where they work (especially if they're your boss).

But like I said, when it ended, I wasn't nearly as devastated as I'd been with others in the past. Take Kylie, for instance (summer of '92); a cute, dressed all in black alterna-chick, cocktail waitress who worked at a local club here. Technically, we never actually dated, though we did sit next to each other at an after-hours party at the club. When I finally got the balls to ask her out, the summer was about over. But she agreed and we went out, and it was nice. Well, at least I thought it was nice. We even kissed goodnight (like really kissed).

A few days later, she left to go back home to Buffalo. She never said an official or unofficial goodbye, and like an idiot, I never asked for her number. Embarrassingly, I never even caught her last name. That would have come in handy when Facebook would take prominence in the stalking world. Anyway, my point is, besides some at-the-bar conversations and an end-of-the-summer make-out session, Kylie and I never even had a relationship. Yet, when she left without a goodbye, I was devastated. Well, maybe not devastated, but pretty God damned depressed (two mixtapes worth).

Now that you have a little backstory, I'm thinking the basketball court at Short Sands is the perfect place to start this tale of 1995. My friends and I have been playing on the beach courts for as long as I can remember. Our summers consisted of basketball during the day and picking up girls at night; sometimes reversed, sometimes simultaneously.

It was my first time shooting hoops there since my return to town a couple days earlier. Doug suggested a good ole basketball/beach day as a way to get me acclimated back home.

Doug Andrews is one of my closest and best friends, which is why I could see through his whole 'get acclimated' bullshit. He just wanted an excuse to hang out at the beach and to have a trusted wing-man to help pick up chicks. Our other two close friends, Scott and Pete were both in relationships, so they weren't really into being Doug's wingmen.

Doug is the ultimate pickup artist, and I don't mean that in a bad way. He's actually a great guy and an even better friend. I think when people hear the words pickup artist they think of a giant douchebag who scams his way into a girl's pants. Yes, sometimes Doug uses cheesy worn out lines. And yes, he's probably had more one night stands than I can count, but I'll give him credit, he's usually honest and up-front with them regarding his one night intentions. And here in *Vacationland*, the girls that come here are usually just looking for the same.

Fun Fact: The phrase 'What happens in Vegas stays in Vegas' was originally 'What happens in York Beach stays in York Beach.' It was first said by Eleanor (Dolly) DeVille in 1952. Eleanor and a couple other married ladies traveled up to York Beach from Massachusetts for the weekend while their husbands were away on business. After taking one look at all the handsome, single men at the beach, Dolly turned to her friends (Gertrude & Irene) and said, "Remember ladies, what happens in York Beach, stays in York Beach."

Okay, that might be more of an *alternative fact*, but it's a fun alternative fact.

Anyway, back to Doug. He very, very, very rarely gets emotionally attached. Like seriously, I think he's only made one or two mixtapes for girls in his whole fucking life! Two mixtapes?? That's called a Saturday night for me. And technically, one of his mixtapes wasn't even a real mix. It was one song, played over and over and over... on both sides ("One More Try" – Timmy T). That "mix" is my one lone piece of ammunition against Doug and his mixtape jokes.

To Doug's excitement, I agreed to hang out with him down at the beach. He didn't have to work until later that night, and I, well... I didn't have a job yet. We started our day off shooting hoops at the beach courts, and my first shot of the summer of '95 – nothing but net!

"Nice shot, bro," Doug complimented. "Did you play any in Rhode Island?"

"Nope. I haven't even picked up a ball since I left here. Feels good to be back home though."

"I bet," he said. "I'm sorry it's because you and Liz broke up."

I knew in his heart, he was glad to have me back as a girlfriend-free partner in crime, but I also knew he really was sorry about my relationship ending. Doug definitely had a sympathetic, caring side to him.

"Holy shit! Check out the rack on that girl," he exclaimed as he pointed to a young girl heading down the sidewalk towards the courts. He also has a horny, perverted side to him too.

"Dude, she's like seventeen," I whispered.

"No way! She's totally twenty-one-ish. I have a good eye for age," he said as he continued staring (lecherously) at the girl. "They never looked that hot when we were that age, did they? And they never showed that much skin, did they?"

I gave my best non-lecherous gaze up the sidewalk at the outfit in question. She wore a three-size-too-small bikini top and tight, TIGHT Daisy Dukes with long bronze-tanned legs. Doug was a huge perv, but he was a huge perv who spoke the truth. Girls certainly didn't dress like that when we were younger.

"Quick, give me the ball," Doug said. "It's time for the ole runaway ball trick." Without thinking, I handed Doug the ball. He took it and slowly rolled it towards the sidewalk. "A little help, please," he politely yelled to the girl.

She spotted the ball heading for road and quickly rushed (jiggled) over to pick it up. When she bent over to pick it up, her underwear... um, her thong... her bright pink thong... was revealed. My look may or may not have turned a bit lecherous as well.

It's amazing how such a tiny, tiny piece of fabric can turn two semi-adult men into two mesmerized idiots. So mesmerized in fact, that we didn't see her giving us the antiperv-death-stare. And we certainly didn't see her discard our ball into the street. Our zombie-like stares were only broken by the loud sound of our ball getting run over by a green Jeep Cherokee.

"Fuckin' pervs," she snapped and continued down the sidewalk towards the beach.

You might think this little 'runaway ball' trick was stupid and immature, and you'd probably be right, but I tell you this, we have met more girls this way than I can count. Some just ended in conversation. Some led to party invites. And a few even led to… other stuff. All in all, the 'runaway ball' trick probably had a 23% success rate, and in a guy's mind, that was a huge success. This girl, however, was obviously part of the 77% club.

As the girl jiggled and swayed her hips (on purpose I bet) towards the beach, a voice from behind us called, "You guys wanna play two on two?"

We turned back around to see two pimply-faced teenagers standing there wearing Chicago Bulls jerseys (Scotty Pippen & Michael Jordan).

"Young guns against the old guys," said the prepubescent white Jordan.

"Old?" I scoffed. "We're like twenty-five. That's hardly old."

"To be fair," said Doug, "we probably seem old to them. What are you guys, like fifteen?" Both kids nodded. "See, I told you Josh, I have an eye for age. Alright young guns, let's see what you got."

Before the game started, the pimply-faced white Pippen smirked, "You do know the chick that popped your ball was only fifteen, right?"

I immediately felt dirty... and old. And yeah, like a fuckin' perv.

"What were you saying about having an eye for age?" I said to an equally stunned Doug.

"Don't even start with me," snapped Doug. "You were staring too."

He was right, of course, so I figured it was just best that we dropped it and concentrated on beating these two young punks. And beat them we did. I'm a naturally competitive person by nature, but after falling behind nine to one to them, I got pissed and made it my personal mission to shut these two young, cocky motor-mouthed, homeboy wannabes up!

After every made basket, it was the same tiresome comments. "Pippen to Jordan! Jordan to Pippen!" That was followed with some lame handshake or fist bump crap.

For as much as Doug likes to talk shit, and yes, he loves to talk shit, he was surprisingly quiet. We both were. It was obvious that we were embarrassed that these two clowns were schooling us. The turning point came when I faked and blew by pimply-faced Pippen and headed in for an easy layup attempt. I say attempt because out of nowhere, jack-hole Jordan flew in and blocked my shot. Badly. And if that wasn't embarrassing enough, he followed it up by wagging his finger in my face exclaiming, "Not in my house, bitch!"

Let me just put this out there, I'm definitely not a violent person. A lover not a fighter, if you will. That being said, I wanted to punch this douche-dick square in the throat. I'm not sure what I was offended by more, being called a bitch or him claiming this was 'his house.' His house? Are you shitting me? It was obvious by his loud, annoying accent that he was not from around here; the Boston area I'm thinking, but either way, definitely a Mass-hole.

His house? Ha! I've been playing on these courts for as long as I can remember, and these idiot tourists come to our beach for two months a year and think they have the right to call this their house? Where the hell were they in the middle of winter, when we'd freeze our asses off shoveling the court just to play for an hour or so? Huh??

So, I didn't punch him in the throat, and I didn't even respond to him verbally. Instead, I glared over at Doug, and without saying a word, we read each other's mind. From that point on, we went on a seventeen to two run and took an eighteen to eleven lead.

Doug and I remained quiet. Our high-fives and fist bumps were only communicated in our minds. Needless to say, the Mass-holes' yapping picked up considerably. But this time, their yapping wasn't directed at us, but rather at each other. The Jordan/Pippen honeymoon was most definitely over!

3

"MELT WITH YOU" – Modern English

After Doug and I took care of the not-so dynamic duo, we decided to call it a day and hit the beach for a bit. Considering it was mid-morning, the beach at Short Sands was already nearly filled to capacity. We found ourselves a little real estate on the far edge of the beach, directly behind the two young girls renting the Fun Floats. "Bob's Fun Floats," to be exact.

Sitting with the girls were two equally young dudes. They weren't their boyfriends, but I could tell by their loud, obnoxious show-off banter, that they were definitely trying their best to be.

The sight of the Fun Floats and listening to the boys showing off, brought back a flood of memories. I spent most of my high school summers hanging out with Fun Float girls. Remember Cara Montgomery - my high school crush? You know, the one who got me into The Cure and other alternative bands. You guessed it, she was once a Fun Float girl, and I was once one of those boys. I remember my friends and I spending many a beach day just sitting around hanging out with Cara and her best friend Heather Grant. Between all the beaches in York, there were probably five or six float stands, but it was at this very one that I listened to the Cure's "Standing on a Beach" tape for the first time.

Before I had the chance to remind Doug of our ole fun float-girl-chasing days, I noticed him contentedly scanning the beach. From butts to boobs, to long, tanned, well-oiled legs, he was in York Beach heaven. I didn't have the heart to interrupt his pervy beach scan, so I settled into my beach chair and smiled. It really was good to be back home.

"Psst." Doug nudged my arm and motioned to his right.

Lying face down on a giant towel was a tall, toned, well-oiled body. Her long, flowing blonde hair rested on her back. Doug's eyes (and maybe mine) were fixated on her equally well-toned ass. Her ass was accented by a white thong, which was trying its best to do a disappearing act. Doug nudged me again and pointed out she was sans bikini top.

I didn't have to look at Doug to know what he was thinking. He planned on staring at her as long as it took, in case she sat up abruptly or shifted or adjusted even; all in hopes of catching a quick glimpse of boobage. You would think at the age of twenty-five, our maturity level would have improved, but... well, not so much.

Fortunately, Doug didn't have to wait long. She slowly rolled over, stood up, and faced in our direction. Maybe I should rephrase that sentence. HE slowly rolled over, stood up, and when HE turned around to face us, all HE had on was his white (snug) banana hammock with a Canadian maple leaf on it. Some things in life you just can't unsee.

Still in shock, Doug turned to me and whispered in disgust, "Fuckin' French Canadians!"

Our embarrassment and shock was short-lived, as two girls (two real girls) entered the beach and placed their towels and chairs directly in front of us. I would like to say they were in their twenties, but after the day we've had so far, I didn't even dare to venture a guess.

The one on the left had dirty blonde hair, dark sunglasses, Daisy Dukes, and a blue tank top on. She wasted no time in slipping off her tank and shorts. She then began rubbing lotion on herself. Any second I expected to hear Doug's voice ask, 'Do you need help with that?' But surprisingly, he sat quietly, reclined in his chair with his sunglasses on. It almost appeared like he was sleeping, but I knew better. Behind his dark shades, his eyes were intently watching her continue to lotion herself. When she finished, she climbed into her chair, reclined back fully, and there, to Doug's pleasant surprise, was full-on cleavage. Again, Doug was in York Beach heaven.

While Doug fake-sleep-stared at her, I turned my attention to her friend. She had short brown hair, dark brown eyes, and the cutest blue-rimmed glasses on; regular glasses, not sunglasses. She wore a simple white tee with a cute jean skirt. If it seems like I use the word cute a lot, it's only because that's exactly what she was, cute… super cute.

Through my own sunglasses, I watched as she attempted to unfold her beach chair. It quickly became apparent that she wasn't as graceful as her friend. When she finally unfolded it, she placed her iced coffee in the cup holder and took her tee shirt off. As she pulled her shirt over her head, her glasses got caught and fell into the sand. Embarrassingly, she brushed them off and looked around to see if anyone was watching. Luckily, my eyes were well-hidden behind my glasses.

With her glasses wiped off and put back on, she attempted to slip off her skirt. I say attempted, because they got caught around her ankles causing her to fall into her friends chair. Her friend pushed her back up, smirking at her clumsiness. I couldn't help but to smirk as well. Doug didn't smirk, for the disruption interrupted his perfect cleavage view. What happened next could only be described as the most adorably hilarious, uncomfortable thing I have ever witnessed.

When she finally got her skirt off and 'attempted' to sit in her chair, the chair snapped shut and sent her and her iced coffee crashing into the sand. If that wasn't bad enough, she fell onto the tube of suntan lotion, sending a giant glob of lotion directly onto the French Canadian's grape huggers. His eyes remained shut tight, with no clue that he now had a glob of lotion on his... maple leaf. Her face turned bright red. Her friend burst out laughing. I fought back my own laughter.

"Oh my God," whispered Doug, "are you watching this car crash? That chick is a hot mess."

Another Fun Fact: Although the phrase 'hot mess' wouldn't take prominence until circa 2010, it was indeed spoken by Doug for the first time on that very day in the summer of '95. I can definitely vouch for him on that one. What I can't vouch for is Doug's claim that he started the whole *That's what he said/That's what she said* craze.

Doug quickly noticed my look was less about her being a hot mess and more about her being just hot... in a cute, klutzy sort of way. He shook his head and chuckled at my smitten look.

"Well, go make your move, Romeo," he said.

"I will," I said. "When the moment is right, I will."

Again Doug chuckled, "I'd bring some caution tape with you."

As it turned out, I only had to wait ten minutes for an opening for my move. Ironically, it came from the French Canadian's radio. "I Melt with You" by Modern English blared out and caught the ears of the girls. In particular, the cute one I had my eye on.

"Aw, I love this song," she said. "I can never remember who sings it though. It was one of those one-hit wonders from the 80s."

Her friend shrugged then motioned over to the French Canadian. "Why don't you go ask Frenchy if he knows. And maybe you can give him a *hand* rubbing that lotion in. Although, by the looks of it, you're gonna need more lotion."

Both girls looked over at the glob of lotion still sitting on his well-hung package. It was right then and there, as both girls laughed, that I decided to seize the moment and make my move.

"Modern English," I announced. Both girls looked back at me. "This song… I Melt with You… it's by Modern English. It came out in '82. 1982. It was also featured in the 80s movie "Valley Girl" with Nicolas Cage. Kind of a cheesy movie, but still a classic… kinda."

"Uh, thanks," she said to me.

If I had a cowboy hat on, I would have tipped my hat and said, 'My pleasure, ma'am.' But seeing as I didn't, I simply winked and said, "You're very, very welcome." Of course she didn't actually see me wink because I had sunglasses on.

After they turned back around towards the ocean, I felt Doug staring at me. "What?" I asked.

"That was your move?" he said.

"No. That was my pre-move move," I answered.

My next opportunity to make a move on the cute girl came only seven minutes later. After spilling her entire iced coffee earlier, she was in desperate need of another. She got up, slipped her shirt and skirt back on and told her friend she was going to get another drink. I quickly threw on my shoes and casually followed her off the beach.

As I stood behind her in line, I couldn't help myself, I began whistling "I Melt With You." She turned slightly, but it was just enough for me to see that she was smiling. Wait, was she smiling with me or at me? Just in case in was the latter, I immediately stopped whistling. I watched her approach the take-out window and order.

"Can I have two large iced coffees, please?" she said.

The woman made her drinks, but when she noticed the cute girl was holding a credit card, she said, "I'm sorry, our card machine is down right now. We're only accepting cash. Sorry."

The look on her face said it all. She had zero cash on her.

"Add two more and I'll pay," I jumped in and said.

The woman behind the counter smiled at my amazingly sweet gesture and made two more drinks. The cute girl turned and shyly said, "You don't have to do that."

"It's no problem," I smiled.

If I left it at that, it would have been just fine, but I have a tendency to babble a bit when I'm nervous, or excited, or nervously excited.

"My buddy and I are actually sitting behind you on the beach. I'm the Modern English guy. I mean, I'm the one who told you they sing 'I Melt with You.' I didn't really mean I was the actual Modern English guy. That'd be pretty cool though... although, they were pretty much just a one-hit wonder so maybe that would suck... although, right now I'm a no-hit wonder so maybe being a one-hit wonder wouldn't be so bad. I'm Josh, by the way."

She looked overwhelmed by my babble. She also looked like she was going to point out that I just said the longest run-on sentence in history. But she didn't. Instead, she offered a smile and said, "I'm Elise."

"Cool. That's like one of my favorite Cure songs."

I could tell by her blank look that she had either never heard of the song or never heard of The Cure. Luckily, she was too cute for me to hold that against her.

"You've never heard of them, have you?" I asked.

"I've heard of them. Don't they do that 'Friday I'm in Love' song?" she asked.

Again, luckily she was cute.

"Um yeah," I replied. "That was their big radio hit, but they have so many better songs. So many. The song I was referring to is called 'A Letter to Elise.' It was actually on the same album as that 'Friday I'm in Love' song. The Wish album... 1992. My second favorite Cure record. 1989's Disintegration being the first. Definitely the first."

Sometimes when I start spitting out music facts, I sound an awful lot like Rain Man.

'Disintegration is definitely the best... yeah, definitely the best. It came out in '89...1989.'

I actually had to look down at myself to make sure I wasn't swaying back and forth like Rain Man. Ugh. I'm a total dork. Fortunately, I wasn't swaying.

Is it wrong that I was already thinking where I would place that song on her mixtape? Should I *start* the tape off with it or *cap* it off with it???

She seemed quiet as we walked back towards the beach together. My mind quickly raced for something smart to say. Well, maybe not smart, but at least something funny. I needed it to be short and sweet and not a long, babbling run-on sentence.

I watched her take a sip of her iced coffee and I said, "Try not to spill this one."

Shit! That wasn't smart or funny. It was more sarcastic, if anything.

"Oh my God," she blushed. "You saw that?"

"Right down to the lotion hitting Frenchy's package," I smiled.

She continued to blush, but followed it with a giggle. Relax! It wasn't a 'cute' giggle... just a giggle.

"Self-proclaimed, I'm like the clumsiest girl in the world," she said.

"Eh, it's okay," I said. "Self-proclaimed, I'm like the king of babble. So, are you and your friend here for the week or just day-trippers?"

"The rest of the summer actually. Nikki and I are staying with my grandmother. She has a cottage on one of those side streets up by the lighthouse. I just graduated a couple of months ago."

"From college?" I asked. She looked a bit offended as she

nodded yes. "I assumed so," I said, "but it's hard to tell nowadays. There are fifteen year olds that look twenty-one, for crying out loud. Maybe it's just evolution, or maybe they're drinking more milk… if so, it really *does* do the body good. I'm not saying you look fifteen… or that you don't drink enough milk… I'm just saying…(I had no idea what I was saying)… ummm, are you from around here?"

"Vermont."

"Ah, the Green Mountain State. The Ben & Jerry state. Yeah, you kinda got that Vermont thing going on," I said.

She looked blankly at me. Well, maybe not blankly. More like, 'What the hell are you talking about' kinda look.

"I have no idea what I'm babbling about," I admitted. "Did you go to college in Vermont?"

"No. California."

"Oh cool. Good ole Cali," I said (never having been there).

What happened next, absolutely proved that it's impossible for me to edit my thoughts. For some strange, dorky reason, I started to bust into L.L. Cool J's "Going back to Cali." And by bust into I mean I actually rapped it. This time, her look was truly blank. Blank enough to stop me from bustin' out more rhymes.

"Um… 'Goin' Back to Cali?' The L.L. Cool J song?? I'm dying here, aren't I?" I said.

She smirked and made the *little bit* gesture with her fingers. Luckily for me (and her) we reached our spots on the beach.

"Thanks again for the drinks," she said.

"No, thank you," I answered.

She politely smiled and handed Nikki her drink and sat back down in her chair. As I sat back in my own chair I couldn't help but think, *what the hell was I thanking her for?* Idiot!

I handed Doug his drink then pointed out he owed me for the drinks… for all the drinks. After all, he indirectly caused my basketball to get run over.

He knew he couldn't argue with that, so instead, he quietly asked, "So, how'd it go with the cute klutz?"

Cute was his word NOT mine. I looked over at Elise then gave Doug two thumbs up.

He laid back in his chair, paused a second, then said, "You totally babbled her to death, didn't you?"

This time it was me who gave the *little bit* gesture with my fingers. We both laughed (more him than me).

Sadly, I didn't get another chance that day to talk to her, or flirt, or ramble, or whatever the fuck I do. I went to the bath house to take a piss and when I came back, Elise and Nikki had already packed up and left. I should have used our brief time together to ask her out, or at least what they were doing tonight. Instead, I spent our brief time lamely rapping an L.L. fuckin' Cool J song. Idiot!

***

It was about three o'clock when we started to pack up and

leave the beach. Doug had to head to work at four. When we were teenagers, we both worked in the kitchen at a restaurant around the corner from here. Murphy's Oceanside Restaurant, to be exact. Doug only lasted two summers there. After that, he started working at a bar. Now he's the head bartender at a small bar just over the border in Portsmouth, New Hampshire.

For what seems like years, he's been telling us that he's going to open up his own bar one day back here at the beach. It's always the same conversation; he has an uncle or a cousin, or some relative who is on the verge of funding his dream. I say this not to make fun. Not at all. I think it's great that he knows exactly what he wants to do with his life. I'm more jealous than anything.

From age sixteen to twenty-two, I worked at Murphy's in the summer as well as a few other restaurants in the winter. It was definitely NOT because I loved it. It's just sort of what I did while I waited for what I really wanted to do. That question still remains, by the way.

When I was twenty-three, I vowed to at least try something different. I took a marketing-type job, which is just a fancy way of saying I sat on my ass in a cubicle making cold calls to try and sell people things they didn't even need or want.

Surprisingly, I lasted a whole year there. Mostly, it was because I hate being looked at as a quitter. And because of that fact, I stick things out way longer than I should. It's just another one of my quirks. Finally, I just couldn't deal with the monotony of my meaningless job and I quit. Not to mention, my boss was a major uptight d-bag.

Years later, when I saw the movie "Office Space," I swore I could have written it! Actually, there are quite a few movies out there that I think (wished) I could have written, but that's a subject for another time.

As Doug and I headed down the boardwalk, I heard an older voice call out to me.

"Joshua? Joshua Wentworth? Is that you?"

I turned to my right and there on the bench was my old boss, Mr. Murphy. It had only been a few years since I'd seen him last, but his grey hair was greyer, and his wrinkles now had wrinkles.

"Hey, Mr. Murphy. How are you?" I said shaking his hand.

He quickly turned the shake into a hug. He was always a great boss, and for the most part, we got along, but if I was still his employee, he would have never done the hugging thing. I should have known right then and there something was up.

"Seems like forever since I've seen you around, Josh. Where have you been?"

"Yeah, I needed to try something new. I took a stupid marketing job, but that didn't really pan out. Then last year I worked for a landscaping company, but that ran its course, too. Then I met this girl from Rhode Island and I ended up moving down there last winter. Her father owns a bunch of retail stores, and I tried doing that, but it didn't really work out."

"The job or the girl?" asked Mr. Murphy.

"Both," interjected Doug. "Hey, Mr. M, do you remember me? I used to work for you too... way back. Doug? Dougie Andrews?"

Mr. Murphy's smile faded. He looked Doug straight in the eyes and said, "Didn't I fire you for trying to steal a keg of beer from me?"

Proudly Doug boasted, "Yeah, that was me! I put the keg in a garbage bag and threw it in the dumpster with the other garbage and later that night I came back for it. It woulda worked too, if that stupid rent-a-cop didn't see me dumpster diving. Ahh, good times, good times."

While Doug reminisced with himself, Mr. Murphy turned his attention back to me.

"So, Josh, now that you're back home, where are you working?"

"Um, I'm kind of in limbo right now regarding a job... or a career... or my life. A life limbo, if you will."

With a glint in his eye, Mr. Murphy rubbed his grey beard and said, "Hmmm, I see."

"Ohhh, no, no, no," I said, knowing exactly where this was heading.

"What? You didn't even hear my offer," he smiled.

"Yeah Josh, you didn't even hear his offer," Doug

interrupted.

"I don't want you to just work for me this summer, I want you to manage the place." Before I could ask what he meant, he said, "I've been trying to remove myself for a couple of years now. I'm too old and too tired to be hanging out there as much as I do. Between you and me, I'm probably going to sell the place soon."

"Wow. You've owned that place forever, but... but I'm not sure I could manage the place for you," I said.

"Nonsense! You're the perfect person for the job. You know the place inside and out, and if anyone could handle this year's crew, I know it'd be you."

"Handle?" I asked.

"Yeah, let's just say they are an eclectic bunch. It's only the second week of July and they have already run off four managers this season. One of them pulled your old lobster antics today on my newest manager; now my former manager."

The lobster antics he referred to were implemented three times in my seven years. It was successful twice. Wildly successful once. Back in '91 we had a huge dickhead of a manager. He did nothing all day except try to hit on the waitresses. The only time he acted like he was working was when Mr. Murphy showed up. That's when he turned into Captain Helpful. *'You need me to put more ice on the clams? Of course! You need another case of fries from the freezer? Of course! I'm on it!'*

That's when I came up with my idea. I took a live lobster and removed the bands from its claws and put it inside a box of coffee creamers. We put the box on the top shelf of the refrigerator, which, for our Napoleon-sized manager, was just above his eye level. And just as planned, when Mr. Murphy came in to check on things, Captain Helpful jumped into action trying to be as helpful as possible. Also, just as planned, one of the waitresses yelled to him that she needed more creamers.

Without hesitating, our dickhead manager rushed over to the fridge and reached his hand up into the box for a handful of creamers. To his shock (and our viewing pleasure), the lobster clamped down on his hand. Hard. Really hard. Despite his screaming and flailing around the kitchen like a maniac, the lobster didn't let go. If cell phones and YouTube had been around back then, the lobster incident would have totally gone viral. He'll never admit it, but I swear, even Mr. Murphy cracked a slight smile that day.

As much as I enjoyed reminiscing about past summers' antics, there was no way I was going back to that place to work. Nope, no way.

"I have a good core crew this year," Mr. Murphy said. "Like I said, they're a little strange and eclectic, but they're good kids. They just need a manager that is more relatable to them. My head cook actually reminds me a lot of you, Josh. He has a lot of potential, he just needs to…"

"Apply himself and take his head out of his ass?" I asked.

"I believe you said the exact words to me once upon a time."

"See, that's why you'd be perfect for the job. Besides, there are only six busy weeks of summer left. You can handle that, right?"

When Mr. Murphy gave you a look like that, it was nearly impossible to say no.

"I say go for it," added Doug. "Now maybe I'll be able to collect some rent from your sorry ass."

"I tell you what," Mr. Murphy persisted, "if, at any point this summer you leave for a *real* job, no hard feelings. Deal?"

With both their eyes on me, I finally gave in and said, "Fine. I'll do it."

"Excellent! You start tomorrow at 3pm. Don't be late."

And just like that, he went from begging to being a hardass boss.

As he walked away, Doug called to him, "Hey, Mr. M, if you need a little extra help—"

Mr. Murphy cut him off, "You do know we don't serve alcohol anymore?"

"Oh, forget it then," Doug mumbled.

4

"BIZARRE LOVE TRIANGLE" – New Order

The next day, not only was I not late, but I showed up a half an hour early. Mr. Murphy was out running errands, so I decided to grab a bite to eat and do a little recon of what I was getting myself into. The place was small enough that you only needed two or three waitresses on at a time and maybe three or four in the kitchen.

The décor had a distinctive Maine coast feel to it. There was a lot of rustic woodwork throughout, with plenty of pictures of lighthouses, beaches, and other local attractions. Scattered among the pictures were old buoys and a few lobster traps.

Because the kitchen was closed off to the dining room, I didn't get a chance to check out the kitchen crew, but I was able to watch and eavesdrop on two of the wait staff, Chad and Megan. I couldn't put my finger on it, but Chad looked a little familiar.

They both looked to be twenty or twenty-one. It quickly became apparent that neither of them had an edit button or a *'quiet, there are customers around'* button. It was also apparent that they shared some sort of past together. As they cleared the table next to me, this was the conversation that I heard.

"Hey, Megan, I heard we're getting a new waitress this afternoon."

"Yeah, so." Megan answered.

"I give her one or maybe two shifts before she succumbs to my charm," he arrogantly said.

"Pffft," scoffed Megan, "like you have any fucking charm!"

"If I remember correctly, enough charm to have you sucking my dick on the beach last summer," he boasted.

I was shocked he said that out loud in the dining room with me sitting only five feet away. Luckily, I was the only customer in earshot. By the look on Megan's face, she couldn't believe he said it out loud either. Although, it didn't prevent her from spouting back at him equally as loud.

"I can't believe you're bringing that up!" she snapped. "I was wicked shitfaced that night. And to think, I actually thought you cared about me."

"Yeah," Chad smiled, "that's the beauty of my lines."

This caused Megan's voice to rise up even louder.

"Ya know what, Chad? I fucking despise you! I only still work here because I need the money. So you can go bang the new waitress until her head falls off for all I care!" Megan then stormed into the kitchen, leaving Chad to continue to smile smugly.

The only thing worse than staff drama, is when every single customer hears the drama. And by the look on everyone's faces, they heard loud and clear.

"Doing a little pre-work recon?" a voice from behind me asked. I turned to see old man Murphy standing there smiling. He then motioned in Megan's direction and said, "She's a little loud and straightforward, but she's a good waitress."

"They both seem loud and straightforward," I said.

Mr. Murphy chuckled. "Yeah, my grandson can be quite the spoiled brat sometimes. Most of the time actually."

"He's your grandson? I knew he looked familiar. He used to hang out here my first couple of summers."

Mr. Murphy nodded. "Yup. Then my daughter and my idiot son-in-law moved out to Chicago. They all just moved back last year. For some strange reason, Chad thinks he's going to take over this place from me one day."

"He doesn't really seem like the 'type' for this business," I said.

"Ha," Mr. Murphy laughed, "He's not even the 'type' to

be a waiter." He then looked at his watch and said, "Let me go introduce you to the rest of the crew."

Seeing as it was in between lunch and dinner, three o'clock was usually the big lull at the restaurant. It was a good time to get restocked and ready for the dinner rush. It was also a great time for goofing off.

That being said, I certainly didn't expect to see what I saw when we entered the kitchen. Two of the cooks were just standing there staring up at a fly strip. A fly strip full of flies. They both looked to be in their early twenties.

The taller one had big glasses on and his jeans were ripped in multiple places and patched with... duct tape? His sneakers were huge! They must have been at least a size fourteen. Both toes were completely blown out and patched with, yup, more duct tape. The shorter guy looked more normal... more capable. Their conversation went something like this.

"I'll give you a buck to eat them," said the shorter guy.

"A buck? No way!" scoffed Mr. duct tape.

"A buck for each one," clarified the shorter one.

"Deal!" said the other almost excitedly.

Before I had the chance to witness this fly eating bet, Mr. Murphy waved Megan and Chad over.

"This is my grandson, Chad. And this little firecracker is Megan. Megan, Chad, this is our new manager for the summer, Josh."

My polite *Hello* was drowned out by their looks of disdain. At least Megan tried to fake a welcoming smile. Chad, not so much.

He looked right past me to his grandfather and said, "When this one quits, I say you let me run this place." This caused Megan to roll her eyes and head back into the dining room.

"I think you should just concentrate on the job you were hired for," Mr. Murphy sternly said to Chad.

It was Chad's turn to roll his eyes and storm into the dining room. The one thing I used to hate, but now kind of loved, was how Mr. M never sugar-coated anything.

When our attention finally returned to the two cooks, the taller one was using a toothpick to clean flies out from his teeth. In between picking fly guts out, he proudly exclaimed, "Seventeen bucks! Pay up, Todd!" After Todd paid up, they both made their way over to us.

"Guys, I want you to meet your new manager, Josh. Josh used to be one of my best employees. How long did you work here again?" Mr. Murphy asked me.

"Seven summers," I answered.

"Josh, this is Todd and Phil."

Todd was by far the least receptive of the bunch. He didn't even make eye contact with me. I can't really say I blamed him. I remember the feeling of getting a new manager thrown on us. The last thing we wanted was to give him a fake-welcoming hand shake.

Phil was a little more welcoming. In between picking flies out of his teeth, he offered his huge mitt-of-a-hand and gave me a semi-welcoming shake.

"I've heard about you," Phil said to me. "You're like a legend round here."

"Ha, I don't know about that," I said.

I was torn between being proud or being embarrassed. I didn't have a chance to decide, as Mr. Murphy ushered me over towards the sink area.

The person who was running the dishwasher can only be described as colorful and animated. He was the same age as Todd and Phil but was dressed nothing like them. He wore bright pink shorts. Bright, *tight* pink shorts. Around his forehead he wore a powder blue sweat band and had on a vintage '84 Madonna t-shirt. He also had on a pair of black oversized headphones attached to a Walkman on his hip to which he was jamming and singing along to "Cruel Summer" by Bananarama. When he noticed us standing there, he slipped off the headphones and pranced over to us. Literally.

"This is your new manager, Josh," announced Mr. Murphy. And Josh, this is…"

"I'm Freddy – dishwasher extraordinaire!" he sang. Literally. "And I can bus tables like nobody's business!"

Now I swear I'm not being stereotypical when I say he did some sort of bow/courtesy thing in front of me.

He then limply shook my hand and excitedly said, "My close friends call me Merc… as in Freddy Mercury of Queen."

"Nobody calls you that," Megan said as she walked by.

Freddy gave her an embarrassed stare-down, composed himself, then said to me, "Anyway, I think Queen is the greatest band in the world!"

"Bananarama isn't too shabby either," I joked.

Freddy's eyes lit up as he said, "You like Bananarama?"

"Are you kidding?" I smiled. "I love all 80s music."

Freddy fanned himself as he gushed, "Me too, me too! I totally heart the 80s!"

"And "Cruel Summer" is a classic," I said. "Released in the UK in '83 and in the U.S. in '84. Also made famous by the movie…"

"*The Karate Kid*," we said together.

Freddy turned to Mr. Murphy and beamed. "I like this guy a lot!"

After the interestingly awkward introductions, Mr. M motioned me to follow him into his little office in the back. As we walked off, I heard Todd loudly mumble, "Pfft, legend my ass."

Yup, it was official. I had joined the dark side, otherwise known as management. Mr. M sensed my apprehension and gave me his best attempt at a pep talk. He also made it clear that I had full reign of the place; hiring, firing, scheduling, ordering, etc. He also made it clear the less he had to step foot in this place this summer, the better.

He then jotted down a figure and handed it to me. It was my weekly salary. I'm not going to reveal exactly what it was, but let's just say, great compensation always trumps great apprehension. Always. With that, he headed out to go golfing and left me to deal with the zoo known as Murphy's Oceanside Restaurant.

When I reentered the kitchen, I immediately felt Todd's eyes glaring at me. I could also sense his wheels turning, thinking of all the ways to run me outta Dodge. Before his laser-like glare burned a hole in my skull, Megan entered the kitchen and approached me.

"Hey bossman, the new waitress chick is out in the dining room. Our last manager hired her before he had a little run in with Larry the lobster." Everyone in the kitchen smiled with Megan. "Anyway, you might wanna go save her before Chad sinks his teeth, or whatever else into her. Although, if you don't want to bother, I'm sure we'll have a new manager tomorrow anyway."

"Ahh, this is what Mr. Murphy meant by firecracker," I said as I exited the kitchen.

I took two steps into the dining room then stopped dead. There, standing with Chad was the new waitress… AKA, Elise from the beach yesterday. Our eyes met at the same time, and we shared a look. Not the same look, mind you. Mine was more of an *Aww, this is such a happy coincidence* (in a smitten overtone). Hers was more like, *Aw shit. Just my dumb luck* (not-so-smitten).

I noticed that Megan was right; Chad had wasted no time in trying to charm her, or more specifically, trying to impress her.

As I moved closer, I overheard Chad say, "So, did I mention my grandfather owns this place? Yeah, he's probably gonna pass this place on to me soon."

I found myself siding with Megan more and more. This guy really was a giant douchebag. Chad turned around when he noticed her looking over her shoulder at me.

"Oh, hey," Chad said to me unenthused. "This is our new waitress. I was just showing her around. If you want, I can train her today. We kind of already bonded a bit anyway."

The look on Elise's face was priceless. I fought back my own laughter and said to Chad, "Thanks, Chad, but I'm thinking I'll have Megan train her today."

I'm not going to lie, I took great pleasure seeing his disappointed, pissed off look.

Chad didn't go down without a fight. "Whatever Megan teaches you, just do the opposite and you'll be fine."

Chad shot me a quick look then sulked off. I almost had my own wiseass comment to throw his way, but then I remembered I was the manager now. I needed to take the high road... for now. And besides, the frickin' cute chick from the beach was my new waitress! I found her application and joined her at one of the tables. I needed something cool and funny to open up the conversation.

"Well, well, well, this is quite serendipitous, huh?" I smiled.

Okay, maybe not so cool... or funny, but it was true.

I read through her application aloud, "Elise Marie Carlile.

Says here you can only work until Aug 30th?"

"Yeah, I have a job lined up in September."

"Back in Cali?" I asked. And although I was again tempted, I just smirked and said, "Don't worry, no more L.L. Cool J rappin' from me."

My comment made her laugh. Well, maybe not laugh, laugh, but it was definitely a smile with a sound.

"No, it's back in Vermont." she said.

I could have sat there and talked to her all day, but I figured that wouldn't be very managerial of me. Not to mention, the longer we chatted, the better the chance I would have babbled something stupid... something that would have made her smile *not* make a sound. So, I left her in the hopefully capable hands of Megan, and I headed into the kitchen.

I didn't say a word. I just wondered around observing. More than anything, I was just trying to get acclimated with the kitchen again. I could tell Todd felt differently. To him, I was watching, waiting for them to screw something up. It was Phil who broke the silence.

"Hey bossman, is it true that you used to be able to flip a burger to the ceiling and catch it behind your back in a bun? Blindfolded?"

"You heard about that, huh?' I couldn't help but laugh.

"Is it true?" Freddy interjected. Hesitantly, I nodded. "Show us! Show us!" Freddy clapped.

"Nah, that was long time ago," I said.

"Oh come on," Todd said, throwing a burger on the grill. "Let's see the legend in action."

I knew his look all too well. Not only did he want me to fail miserably, but he definitely had something else up his sleeve. I wasn't sure what exactly, but I could sense something was up when he motioned to the sole spatula by the grill. I say sole because there are usually three spatulas there. It was obvious he wanted me to pick up that particular one. I simply smiled and walked off.

"See, I told you guys. Legend my ass!" Todd said as I made my way into the office.

As I sat in the office chair, I knew Mr. Murphy was right, Todd did remind me of me. I was never as brash as him though. I was more quietly sneaky. But either way, I remember attempting to run off many a new manager. So once again, I had two choices: I could take the managerial high road and ignore their antics, or I could beat them at their own game. I did mention I was competitive, right??

With a stool in my hand, I reemerged from the office and headed back towards the crew. I placed the stool by the grill and said to Todd, "Have a front row seat and let's see if I still got it."

Todd sat on the stool, and with a devious grin, he again motioned to the sole spatula. I slowly reached for it but stopped short. With my own devious grin, I reached in my back pocket and pulled out another spatula.

"I don't leave home without it," I smiled.

The guys looked disappointed, especially Todd. By now, Chad and the girls had made their way into the kitchen. With a bun in my left hand and the spatula slid under the burger, I motioned to Freddy to blindfold me, which he excitedly did. I took a deep breath, channeled my inner *legend,* and flipped the burger in the air. My left hand swung behind me and waited... and prayed. And after what seemed like an eternity, I felt the greasy burger slam down on the bun. Bullseye!

Most of the crew had stunned (yet impressed) smiles on their faces. Not Todd... or Chad. I handed the blindfold back to Freddy. I handed the burger to Todd then casually walked back into the office. Todd angrily slammed the burger into the garbage then attempted to stand up. I say attempted because he found his ass was super glued to the stool.

"What the fuck?!" he yelled.

The entire staff burst out laughing as Phil blurted out, "He glued your ass to the stool! He *is* legendary."

Freddy was clapping rapidly and giggled, "I smell summer shenanigans!"

I shut the office door, swiveled around in Mr. M's chair, and victoriously murmured, "Yup, I still got it."

5

"MIXTAPE" – Brand New

After my first official day back at Murphy's, I drove over to the downtown Portsmouth bar where Doug was working, for a well-deserved beer. At the door, I was greeted by Big Mo. I mentioned early that I used to be a DJ. Mo and I used to work there together. The dance club was called Goodnight Ogunquit. It was located in York, but directly on the border of the next town up, Ogunquit. From '90 – '94, I was the Sunday night summer DJ there and Big Mo was one of the bouncers.

He definitely lived up to his name. Not only was he big in stature, but also in personality. Mo looked intimidating, but in truth, he was just a big teddy bear. He was so big, that one time he playfully poked his finger in my chest and I had a bruise for two weeks. That's one tough teddy bear.

The club was sold last fall and turned into something else. Mo and I stood there reminiscing about all the wild and crazy times we had there over the years. We especially reflected on the club's epic final night. The place was jammed packed and every employee was armed with cans of whipped cream and super-soakers. They all took turns climbing up into the DJ booth and spraying the crowd... especially the girls... especially the ones in white shirts. Between balloons, beach balls, and blow up dolls being passed around, the place was insane. Mo and I both agreed how much we missed it already.

As soon as I sat at up at the bar, Doug slid me a Sam's Summer and asked, "So, how was your first day back?"

"Long and eventful," I said, taking a big sip. "One of the cooks tried the ole super glue on the spatula trick on me."

"Ahh, how'd that work out for ya?" Doug asked.

"He obviously didn't see the ole super glue on the stool trick coming," I proudly smiled. Doug offered a solid fist bump.

"Hey, I meant to tell you, guess who I saw in here a couple of weeks ago?" asked Doug. "Good ole Jane Wheeler."

"Really? I haven't seen or talked to her in almost two years," I said. "She's here for the summer?"

"Nah. She was visiting her parents at their summer place. I

guess she landed some job over in London for a record company."

"Record company? Doing what?" I asked.

"Apparently, she's gonna be the official tour photographer for a couple of their bands. Nobody that we've heard of, but she seemed pretty excited. Aren't you gonna ask how she looked?"

I just gave him an indifferent shrug.

"She looked good. She was asking about you."

"What did you say?"

"I told her you were shacking up with some chick in Rhode Island," Doug said then headed over to take someone's order.

The backstory with Jane Wheeler is... well, maybe I'll save that for the next chapter.

When Doug returned, I decided to change the subject from Jane back to the restaurant.

"Dude, you'll never guess who started working at Murphy's today," I said.

"Umm, you?" Doug stupidly said.

"Besides me, you idiot!"

Before I could fill him in, I was greeted with a firm smack on my back. I turned to see another one of my best friends, Pete.

"Welcome home, bro!" he said giving me a big hug.

"Good to be home," I said looking over his shoulder. "Where's Michelle?" I asked.

"She just ran to the bathroom. She'll be right out."

No sooner did he say that, I spotted Michelle heading towards the bar with a huge smile on her face. She rushed over and gave me a big hug.

"You're home!" she said. "We've missed you."

"I missed you guys, too," I said looking at all three of them.

Doug already had a Heineken and a red wine waiting for them as they sat in the stools next to me.

"Is Scott coming down too?" asked Doug.

"Yeah," Pete answered. "He was just waiting until Lauren got out of work."

"You haven't met her yet, have you?" asked Michelle.

"No, not yet. Is she nice?" I asked.

Both Pete and Michelle nodded. "Super nice," Michelle said. "Kinda quiet and shy though."

"I heard you got sucked back into the Oceanside, huh?" smiled Pete.

I sighed and slowly nodded.

"Hey," interrupted Doug, "you were about to tell me who else started working there today?"

"Oh yeah," I beamed. "That Elise girl from the beach yesterday. You know, the one I was flirting with."

"You call that flirting?" Doug laughed. "How old is she anyway?"

"She's twenty-two. Why?"

"Just making sure she was old enough for ya."

Pete and I looked at each other. Pete shook his head and said to Doug, "Last summer you banged a seventeen year old at Mark's party, remember?"

Doug got very defensive. "First of all, we didn't bang. We just fooled around. And second, she told me she was twenty! What am I supposed to do, ID every girl before I hook up with them? It wasn't until the next day that she told me the truth."

"But you banged her the next night too," Pete said laughing.

"Shut up, Pete! I told you, we didn't bang. I just let her give me a blow job, that's all."

"Ohhh, you let her?" laughed Michelle. "Wow, that was very nice of you. I hope she sent you a thank you card."

"Make fun all you want, but all I can say is despite her age, she was way ahead of her time. She mighta had braces, but she gave a BJ like a champ. No raking, scratching, or pinching. Such a smooth ride. It was like the Cadillac of blow jobs."

The visual alone was enough to shut all three of us up.

A little backstory: Doug, Pete, and Scott and I have been friends for what seems like forever; through ups and downs, through thick and thin. By the time that summer of '95 rolled around, we had already created more crazy memories at this beach than some people have in a lifetime.

We all met Michelle in the summer of '90. Michelle, Pete, and Doug were all lifeguards. She immediately became one of our large, core group of summer friends.

She and Pete hit it off right away. And by that I mean, they had sex within a week of knowing each other. They spent that first summer as 'hook up buddies'. No attachment, no commitment, and no problem with the other one 'hooking up' with other people.

When summer ended and they both went back to college, it was like nothing ever happened between them. I don't even think they stayed in touch the whole school year. But when the next summer came around, they picked up right where they left off. Although, this time, as the summer rolled on, it was apparent that they were both falling for each other. By the time Labor Day came, things were very serious. Their final college year was spent in full commitment status.

Seeing them together, how they interact with each other, how they truly love each other, I couldn't help but feel jealous. I was extremely happy for them, but utterly jealous.

Just then, Scott and his new girlfriend, Lauren walked in. After our introductions, we all sat up at the bar. The gang was back together. Before we got too carried away with drinking and reminiscing, Michelle sweetly offered her concern for me.

"Hey Josh, I'm sorry things didn't work out for you and Liz."

Everyone else nodded in agreement.

"Thanks," I said, "but I'm fine. Surprisingly, I'm not that broken up by it."

"Obviously not," announced Doug. "You're already

flirting with that Elise chick. And I use the word flirting lightly."

I dismissed Doug's comment and continued, "I know it sounds bad that I'm not all broken up about it, but it just ran its course, for both of us. It was totally a mutual and amicable breakup. Sometimes that's the way things are meant to be."

As I looked up, everyone (except Lauren) was giving me a blank look.

Before I get to their blank looks, let me clarify something. Was the breakup mutual and amicable? Yes. Am I fine with that? Yes. I really am. But what I left out to my friends, with good reason, was Liz and I actually broke up back in February. The day before Valentine's Day.

Fun Fact: I have never had a girlfriend on Valentine's Day. For whatever reason, things always ended before then. This one certainly pushed the limits but fell ten hours short.

I wasn't worried about my friends making fun of that particular circumstance, but what I was worried about was them questioning, if we broke up in February, why did it take me five months to move out and move back to York?

The sad and pathetic truth was that I felt bad about leaving her high and dry with the rent, so I told her I'd stay until she found a roommate. That wasn't the pathetic part. Within a few weeks of our mutual breakup, she started seeing someone else. There was a natural jealousy, of course there was, but it wasn't because I wanted her back... because I didn't.

The first few weeks she was careful not to bring him around in front of me. I appreciated that. So much so, that I made the idiotic mistake of telling her it didn't bother me if she did.

What. Did. I. Do?

I spent the better half of May and June listening to them... and I don't mean listening to them talk. My Walkman couldn't go loud enough. One time, after they finished their *third* session, I passed him in the hallway, and I shit you not, he offered me a congratulatory high-five. After I high-fived him back, I promptly moved out.

As you can see, there's no way I can give my friends this kind of ammunition. They have enough on me already. Okay, back to their blank stares...

"Who are you and what have you done with Josh?" Pete said.

"What are you talking about?" I said.

"*Sometimes that's the way things are meant to be?*" Pete laughed. "Amicable or not, the Josh I know would be a little more... affected by a breakup."

"Affected?" I repeated.

"Oh for Christ sake!" Doug interrupted. "What Pete is trying to say, is when it comes to breakups or unreturned feelings, you're a sad, depressing sack of shit!"

I looked over to Pete to confirm this information.

Pete shrugged and smirked, "He's paraphrasing of course, but yeah, you have been known to go overboard in your lamenting of relationships."

Before I could defend myself, Doug blasted another shot.

"Pfft, Josh goes overboard even when it's not a relationship." Pete and Scott nodded in agreement.

"You guys are totally exaggerating," I said.

"Oh really?" said Doug. "I have three words for you: Depression Session Mixes."

This caused some snickering from the guys and Michelle.

"How many volumes are you up to now? Six?" asked Pete.

I just glared at them but kept my mouth shut. Partly because I didn't have a good comeback, and partly because, well, I was actually up to volume eight. Don't judge.

"What's a Depression Session Mix?" Lauren quietly asked.

Who the hell brought her? I wanted to ask. But I didn't. I simply buried my face in my beer and awaited someone to fill her in. That someone would be Scott.

"Whenever Josh gets his hopes dashed or his heart broken, he makes mixtapes filled with sad, depressing songs which he entitles *Depression Session*. There'd be many a night... or day, when we'd go over to his apartment..."

"AKA the Dungeon of Doom," added Doug.

"And we'd find Josh just sitting there," continued Scott, "shades pulled, candles lit, incense burning..."

"A bottle of Barcardi in his hand, and the melancholic sounds of The Cure or The Smiths singing to Josh their mournful lullabies from one of his Depression Sessions," finished Pete.

58

And that, my friends, are my Depression Sessions in a nutshell. A blunt, unflattering nutshell, but a nutshell nonetheless.

"And that's not even including all the mixes he makes for girls," added Scott.

"I think it's sweet," Michelle said as she gave me a one armed hug. "How come you've never made me a mixtape?" she said glaring at Pete.

Doug interjected, "You'll need to dump him and break his heart first, and then he'll make you one. Isn't that how it works, Joshy?"

Once again, I didn't bother dignifying a response. And once again, one of my friends dignified one for me.

"No, Doug," began Scott, "you've got it all wrong. Mixtapes for girls come when you're trying to woo them; Depression Session mixes come when you've been dumped."

"Okay guys, enough," warned Michelle. "The poor guy just got back into town. Believe it or not, Josh, they missed you a lot."

"Yeah, yeah, yeah," I said forcing a forgiving smile.

The subject was dropped, and we moved on with our drinking and laughing. The truth was, they weren't wrong. I really was the king of the mixtape. And I suppose my depression sessions were a bit... over the top? But to be fair, I find that listening to sad music when depressed can be very cathartic... in a sad sack of shit sort of way.

Michelle used this lull in the conversation to give Pete a

look. He smiled and nodded.

"Everyone, Pete and I have some big news," announced Michelle.

I'll cut to the chase, Michelle proceeded to show off her new ring... her new engagement ring. Pete went and proposed to her last night without even running it by us. Don't get me wrong, I highly approve of them together, but still, he could have at least mentioned he was thinking of asking her, no?

Scott was the first to give them a congratulatory hug, followed by me. Doug just stared over at Pete and said, "What's up with that? You couldn't even give your friends a heads up, dude?"

"He doesn't need to run everything by us, Doug," I quickly and hypocritically said.

I guess hearing Doug say what I was thinking actually made me realize how stupid my thinking was. Bottom line, their news really didn't come as a shock to us. We knew it was only a matter of time before they tied the knot.

What did come as a totally shock to us was when they informed us they were moving to Florida. Apparently, Pete was offered some job at an up-and-coming computer internet company. To be honest, I wasn't that depressed because I knew this whole 'computer' thing would just be a flash in the pan. But still, the fact that they were not only getting married, but were moving as well, made me realize how things in our group were changing.

6

"NO ONE IS TO BLAME" – Howard Jones

(Jane Wheeler)

As you probably guessed, Jane and I have a history together. A slightly strange history, but an interesting one nonetheless. Jane and I met in the summer of 1990. I had seen her around before, but we never ran in the same circles. During the summer of 1990 our circles would cross.

Scott was working at the York Harbor Inn that summer, and as luck would have it, so was Jane. He invited her and her friends to one of our many summer parties. Jane and I immediately hit it off. She was full of life and energy... lots of energy. We had similar tastes on everything; music, movies, views on life, and even the same twisted sense of humor.

Her summer crew ended up mixing with our crew quite a bit that summer. We would hang out for hours, just talking and laughing together. Although we spent much of the summer together, we never hooked up. To be honest, I was too unsure to ever make a move. I'm usually pretty good about knowing if a girl is into me or not, but with Jane it was tricky. She was so friendly and energetic with everyone, so I just couldn't get a good read on if she liked me; like, LIKED me liked me.

I was having such a great summer hanging out with her that I was scared if I made a move and was rejected, it would ruin what we had built. I wasn't this hesitant with most, but Jane wasn't most. It wasn't until the final party of the summer that I made my move, and to my surprise, my move was successful.

I'll keep the details of that night to myself, but I will say, I left the party the next day on top of the world. Yup, on top of the world until... I started to do that whole over-analyzing thing I tend to do.

1) Did she hookup with me because she was drinking?

2) Did she hookup with me because it was the final party of the summer?

3) Did she hookup with me because she wanted to all along?

4) Does this mean she wants us to be more than friends? If so, then I'm all in!!!

As you can see, not only do I babble and over-analyze

things, I also like to make lists.

Sadly, I concluded it was probably 1 and 2, and because of that, I felt awkward. So awkward, that I never even said goodbye to her before she left for college the next day. I never even got her number or address either.

Like I said before, in the pre-Facebook, Twitter, cell phone days, it wasn't uncommon to go a whole winter not talking to your 'summer friends' once they left the beach. If you really wanted to stay in touch, you needed to get either their home/college number or their address so you could write them a letter. Like a real stamps and envelope type letter.

I thought about Jane often that winter. I knew which college she went to, and I was tempted on multiple occasions to drive there with flowers (and a mixtape?) and search her out, but, well, that just seemed creepy, even for me. Not to mention, Doug kept reminding me that flowers and mixtapes were on the "kiss of death" list.

By the time the summer of 1991 finally arrived, I was bursting at the seams to see and talk to her again. My first opportunity came at a party at a mutual friend's house. By the time Jane showed up, I was six beers in, which meant my heart was fully on my sleeve and my mouth was ready to go.

I wasted no time in telling her how much I missed her this past winter and how I'd been kicking myself for never getting her number or address. Maybe it was the six beers or maybe it was because so much time had gone by, but I proceeded to lay out my feelings honestly and concisely (more honestly than concisely).

I explained why I never said goodbye and why I never asked for her number. I told her I just assumed she thought the whole thing was either a mistake or just an end-of-the-summer hookup. I also made it clear to her that to me it was neither one of those.

As soon as I revealed to Jane exactly how I felt about not only the 'hookup', but how I felt about her, I felt extremely relieved. I'm sure there was some babbling involved, but for the most part, I revealed exactly how I felt about her, the hookup, and how I would love for us to be more than friends.

After I laid this all out there, she became quiet... too quiet. When she finally found the words to speak, she proceeded to reveal her own thoughts to me. I'll summarize them in a list:

1) Not only did she NOT regret our hookup, but she too had hoped that we would have stayed in touch throughout the winter.

If her revelations ended there, I would have been super-happy! But they didn't.

2) Because I didn't ask for her number or even say goodbye to her, she just assumed I looked at that night as a just an end-of-the-summer thing... just another notch on Josh's bedpost, so to speak.

I felt horrible when she told me this, but I also felt pretty positive. This was all just a big, silly miscommunication between us. Bottom line is we both felt the same feeling towards one another. That's a good thing. A fuckin' great thing!!!

Once again, if her revelations ended there, I would have been very happy. But they didn't. Revelation #3 was a killer.

3) Because I never attempted to stay in touch, and because she assumed I looked at her as just another conquest, she had 'mentally moved on' with her life. And because she had mentally moved on, it allowed her to meet and fall in love with some dude named Brandon.

Yes, she used the phrase 'fall in love'. I do believe it was at that point when I thought – *Fuck MY Life*! And just like that, on June 3rd, 1991, the phrase *FML* was born. That's my claim and I'm sticking to it.

Once Jane learned how I truly felt about her all along, she felt horrible. And of course I felt horrible because, well, there was now a dude named Brandon in the picture. It sucked. The whole thing fuckin' sucked. Neither of us could be mad at each other, but just because no one was to blame, it didn't make the situation any better.

So, the summer of '91 was known as the summer of Brandon and Jane. Despite that, however, Jane and I weren't done. It was extremely awkward at first, but we remained close friends, and over the years, we would have several more chances at a relationship. Unfortunately, the story was always the same – bad timing.

7

"KISS OFF" – Violent Femmes

The thing about working at restaurant is there is no such thing as an uneventful day. Day two at Murphy's proved that to be true. Usually, when I wake up on a work day, I have that sick, dreaded feeling about coming into work. I think we've all felt that. On day two however, I felt an eagerness to come in. The fact that Elise was working might have had something to do with it. That same feeling reminded me of when I worked here in the summer of '88.

I think 1988 was my third year at Murphy's, so I wasn't yet high on the totem pole, but I certainly wasn't the lowest. No matter where you were on the totem pole, coming into work on a summer's day always sucked. Having a crush on Aimee Cohen made it suck less. The summer of '88 is when the crush baton was passed from Cara Montgomery to Aimee Cohen.

At the age of eighteen, I hadn't yet hit my flirting prime, so my flirts were more awkward and juvenile. I'm not talking about yanking on her pigtails kind of juvenile flirting, more like lame attempts at humor or showing off. Sadly, Aimee Cohen made it painfully obvious that I was going to be on the 'just friends' side of the coin. And like always, the more obvious she made it, the harder I tried.

I suppose the good news was I didn't embarrass myself, not completely anyway. Aimee and I remained friends for the next few summers, and then, as is always the case in this summer beach town, she just faded away. She may or may not have received a mixtape or three along the way.

I would like to think, in the seven years since, my flirting game had improved, but when Elise showed up with short, tight (& fuckin' cute) pigtails, I felt myself regressing to my eighteen year old self. Don't worry, I didn't pull on her pigtails. I actually didn't even get a chance to compliment her on her look. Chad wasted no time in slouching his arm around her and doing some lame flirting attempt of his own. The only thing worse than watching assholes like Chad flirt, is watching girls like Elise smile and laugh at his stupid lines. I guess it's pretty obvious why they fall for them though; it's his Rob Lowe-esque good looks. The fucker!

I could have butted in and told Elise I needed to go over some things, but I let Chad have his moment. Besides, there was no way a nice girl like Elise would fall for his lines, right? Right?

I decided to just wander about doing important managerial-type stuff. I did get a chance to observe Megan in action. She definitely waited on her customers with a straightforward, open, and honest approach. Maybe too much so. I eavesdropped on her taking an order from a middle-aged couple.

She started with, "Hi guys. How are you today?"

"We're great and you?" the wife replied.

"Well, to be honest," began Megan, "I'm wicked tired. I totally haven't been able to sleep lately. I think I have that amnesia disease."

"Insomnia?" the husband laughed.

"Oh yeah, that one. I always get them confused. I've been staying up wicked late watching TV. You know, late enough to see all those stupid infomercials. It's weird how useful a product can seem at 3am, but not so much after you get it in the mail. Anyway, can I get you two something to drink?"

It quickly crossed my mind if that's how I sounded trying to talk to girls. Nah. Megan finished taking their order and moved on to her next table. I didn't get a chance to hear her comments because I was distracted by Freddy (AKA, the dishwasher extraordinaire). He bounced from table to table busing the dishes, all the while singing, "Come on Eileen".

I've known Freddy for only two shifts, and it was impossible to picture him ever being in a bad mood.

When he saw me watching him sing and dance, he made a gesture to apologize for being loud. He put his finger to his lips as if to tell himself to quiet down. He continued to bounce around, but now mouthed the words rather than singing them aloud.

Megan distracted me from Chad and Elise, and Freddy distracted me from Megan, and now, the person entering the restaurant, distracted me from all of them.

Through the front door walked Geoff Baker; otherwise known as "a little left Geoff". His comments and personality were always a little left of center, hence the name. Now before you go jumping down my throat for making fun of this, I'm NOT! At all! Geoff and I have actually known each other a long, long time, but as you're about to see, you can't help but laugh and shake your head at what comes out of his mouth.

For as long as I can remember, he was a fixture here at the beach. Our town has many colorful characters and Geoff was no exception. He was in his early forties and could always be seen either riding his bike or walking his dog.

He entered wearing wool socks, Hawaiian shorts, and a Jimmy Buffet Cheeseburger in Paradise tank top. At first glance, you might think he was wearing a sweater underneath, but on closer inspection, you'd realize he was just one hairy dude; one hairy and strange dude.

Freddy saw Geoff's entrance and approached me and warned, "Get ready, bossman, here comes our resident cuckoo bird. AKA the Pyro-Dude, AKA the Fart Machine."

I laughed at Freddy's comments, but he was dead on. The two things you could always count on from Geoff were:

1) talking about setting fires.

2) ripping loud farts.

The fire-starter thing I knew was a joke. He would never really do such a thing, but the thought of it definitely amused him. To Freddy's and the crew's surprise, I greeted him by name.

"Geoff! My man! Long time no see."

A serious and surprised look came over his face. "What are you doing here?" he asked. "Did Mr. Murphy die?" he smiled.

He wasn't really smiling at the thought of Mr. Murphy dead, it was just his go-to reaction; that and his laugh.

"Da ha ha ha, Mr. Murphy is dead. Da ha ha ha."

That would be the laugh.

"Are you joking or serious?" he asked. That was one of Geoff's classic catch-phrases.

"No, Geoff, he's not dead. I'm just running this place for him now," I answered.

"Are you joking or serious?" he again asked. Before I could respond, he changed the subject. "Do you remember my dog Jack? We had to put him down last year."

I couldn't resist. "Are you joking or serious?" I said.

"I'm serious."

"Sorry Geoff. Hey, remember when you came to one of my parties and we got Jack drunk on Rolling Rock?"

"That wasn't funny!" he said in a serious tone. "He threw up three times."

Before I could apologize, his serious look turned into a devious laugh.

"Da ha ha ha."

"What's so funny?" I asked.

"Oh, I was just thinking, would you laugh if I burned this place down?" he said pretending to strike a match.

"You haven't changed a bit, have you, Geoff?"

"Yes I have!" he snapped. "I don't talk like that anymore." He paused a second then smiled, "But would you laugh if this place caught fire?"

"No Geoff, I would not."

"Are you joking or serious?"

Are you guys seeing a pattern here? Just then, Megan stepped in and said, "What do you want to eat today, Geoff?"

"Hmmm," he pondered. "How about a hot dog quesadilla with garlic... extra garlic! It helps me fart."

And right on cue, he ripped a loud fart. "Da ha ha ha," he laughed.

"That's disgusting!" scolded Megan. If you're gonna do that, you need to leave."

"Are you joking or serious?" He then proceeded to rip another one in the direction of a family sitting in a booth.

"Out! Now!" I yelled. "And I'm NOT joking, I'm serious!"

I escorted him to the front door, and as the door shut behind him, echoes of *Da ha ha ha* could still be heard. I profusely apologized to the family who got farted on then turned to the wait staff and shrugged, "We go way back."

I decided to escape the dining room and I headed into the kitchen. I assumed Todd would still be pissed about me gluing his ass to the stool yesterday, and the evil glare on his face confirmed my assumption. I wanted to try and straighten things out with him, but I quickly became distracted by Phil's antics over by the fryolators. Rather than skimming the loose fries with a filtered spoon or tongs, he was reaching in the oil with his bare hands; the 350 degree oil.

I cringed. "Jesus Christ, Phil, doesn't that hurt?"

"Eh, a little. Not as much as getting your short hairs ripped off with duct tape though."

I don't know what was worse, the image of that in my head, or the fact he said it completely straight-faced. Actually, the imagery was worse.

"Besides," Phil said, "Todd bet me I couldn't take these out with just my fingers." When Phil's fingers finished bobbing for fries, he proudly yelled to Todd, "Did it! You owe me three dollars and fifty-seven cents!"

I wasn't even going to ask about the low, random figure. Instead, I changed the subject.

"So Phil, what do you do for fun outside of work?'

"I watch TV, play video games, chase squirrels around with weedwackers."

I laughed. Phil didn't.

"You really chase squirrels around with a weedwacker?" I hesitantly asked.

"Squirrels, cats, aardvarks, sometimes aliens." Without laughing or even smiling, he nodded to me and walked over to give Todd a hand.

"He's the nicest guy in the world, but the weirdest." I turned to see Megan behind me. "His topics of discussion usually revolve around squirrels and weedwackers... and duct tape," she said. "He's also known to eat anything for money."

"Good to know. Good to know," was all I could say.

Megan walked over to Todd and Phil and quietly said, "Can you believe Chad is trying to get that new chick to go to a party with him tonight? He's such an asshole."

"I'm telling you," began Phil, "someone should take a weedwacker to his nut sack."

Todd, Megan, and I, all stared at Phil. As Megan left the kitchen, Elise entered; alone, without her new shadow. Finally, I was going to get a chance to talk to her today.

"Hey, rookie," Todd said to Elise. "Word to the wise, stay away from Chad. He's just a player."

Freddy approached and nodded in agreement.

Elise quietly said, "Most guys are, I guess."

Again, Freddy nodded in agreement.

"I guess," Todd shrugged, "but he's bad. Really bad. Last

summer he filled Megan's head with all kinds of sweet talk, only to fuck her and chuck her. Not that Megan is the most innocent girl, but…"

"She's kinda easy," whispered Freddy. "Like Sunday morning easy."

Todd ignored Freddy's comment and said to Elise, "Just a warning, that's all."

Elise appreciatively nodded.

***

Despite dealing with the farting, pyro-talking Geoff and an equally crazy crew, the rest of the day was pretty uneventful. That is, until Chad came bursting into the kitchen about 7pm. Todd was over helping Freddy with the dishes.

Chad marched over to Todd and said, "Hey asshole! What did you say to the new chick?"

"What are you talking about?" Todd answered.

"Earlier, I asked her to go to a party with me tonight. At the time, she seemed quite receptive, but now, out of the blue, she has other plans. Megan denies it was her, so either she's lying or you're the rat. Stay outta my business with the new chick, got it?"

"Hey! She has a name, you know?" interjected Freddy. "It's Elise, and it's a beautiful name."

"I wasn't talking to you, faggot," snapped Chad.

Todd stepped in defending Freddy.

"Watch your mouth, dickhead!" Todd said as he pushed Chad.

As much as I wanted to see Todd punch Chad, I knew I had to act like the manager.

"Alright, guys, back to work," I said in my best managerial voice. And in true manager fashion, I was met by two disapproving glares from Todd and Chad.

The last two hours of the night went by extremely slow. It seemed everybody was pissed at someone or something. Todd and Chad were pissed at each other (& at me). Megan was pissed at the customer who wrote a note on his receipt which said, *Next time, more service and less storytelling!*

I think it was the same customer she was telling about the time she walked in on her boyfriend *banging some blonde bimbo*. Hmmm, maybe the customer had a point.

By the time we were officially closed, the place and the workers were quiet. Too quiet. I could totally sense something was about to go down. And just as I expected, there was yelling coming from the back room. It was Chad.

"Shit! Shit!" he yelled as he approached me holding his wallet. "I left my wallet in my sweatshirt pocket in the back room. I had a hundred dollar bill in here and now it's gone." Chad turned his attention to Todd. "You took it didn't you?"

"Yeah, right," Todd scoffed. "I didn't touch your fuckin' money."

"I always warned my grandfather that you were a crook."

"You son of a bitch!" Todd yelled as he raced towards

Chad.

Before they could go at it, Phil and Freddy broke it up. Well, Phil broke it up. Freddy just covered his eyes and screamed, "Stooooop!"

Todd looked over at me. I still had no idea what to think about this whole thing. Todd then looked over to Freddy and said, "Go ahead, Freddy, check my pockets."

Todd raised his hands in the air as Freddy happily dug his hands into Todd's pockets... thoroughly.

"My pockets don't go that deep, you idiot!" Todd said as he smacked Freddy's hand. Freddy smiled and pulled out his hand. It was empty.

"See, I told you. I didn't take your money," said Todd.

Chad's eyes immediately looked over at Todd's backpack hanging up.

"Oh for Christ sake," Todd said, shaking his head. "Go ahead, Freddy, check it," insisted Todd.

In the main part of the bag, there was just some random clothes. Freddy reached into the front pocket and pulled out keys and a pack of gum. After taking a piece for himself, he dug back in and pulled out a pack of condoms.

"Ooooo," Freddy glowed, "ribbed, for her pleasure." Everyone except Todd smiled at this. Todd snatched them from Freddy's eager hands and glared at him to continue searching. Freddy giggled then continued digging through the other pockets. His giggle quickly faded and a serious look came over his face as hand pulled out a fresh hundred dollar bill. The whole crew stood there shocked, including myself.

"See, I told ya! Fire his ass," Chad smugly said.

That was the final straw, Todd again lunged at Chad. Before his hands could grab Chad by the throat, Phil and I broke it up.

"Alright, enough!" I yelled. I actually yelled, and I never yell. "I don't know what plans you all have, but employee meeting... NOW!"

After everyone sighed loudly, Todd snatched his backpack and announced, "You can count me out. I fuckin' quit!"

Dramatically, Freddy covered his mouth with both hands and watched in disbelief as Todd stormed out.

***

Part of me felt bad for ordering an emergency employee meeting, so I decided to at least make it more casual, more cool. I moved the meeting from the dining room to the Aqua Lounge around the corner. The Aqua Lounge was a small bar/club across the street from the beach. It was pretty much the only dance club in town.

Two things were its claim to fame: On Thursday nights they did quarter drafts... as in twenty-five cents. But even bigger than that, Monday and Tuesdays were eighteen years old and under nights.

York is more of a family-type beach, so there are tons of teenyboppers who live for those nights. Yes, my friends and I used to be some of them. And yes, we were known to bust a move or two. Don't judge. Like I said earlier, dancing/showing off on the dance floor was another great way to *meet* girls. The success-rate percentage for this method was way higher than the runaway ball trick.

My emergency meeting fell on a Wednesday, so the Aqua Lounge was fairly quiet, and we all sat in a big table in the back. It was obvious that no one wanted to be here, including me. But I knew if I didn't say anything now, it would only get worse. And no matter how much money Mr. Murphy threw at me, it wouldn't be worth this giant headache.

Before we were even seated, Chad was already flirting with the cocktail waitress. As I sat down, I thought of Mr. Murphy's words of wisdom to me: *When making a big decision, make sure it's based on what's best for the business and not what's best for you.* Luckily, in this instance, the answer would prove to be a win-win for both.

"Hi guys," the waitress greeted, "How are we doing tonight?"

"Good," I was the only one to answer. I handed her my credit card. "Can you start a tab for me?"

Seeing this, Chad blurted out, "Yeah! That's what I'm talking about." He then winked at the waitress.

I knew what I needed to do.

"Whatever everyone wants," I told her. "Everyone except him," I said pointing to Chad. "You're fired."

I didn't even have to look to my right to know Freddy was

bug-eyed and covering his mouth in shock.

"Yeah, right," Chad laughed.

His stupid, cocky smile faded when he realized I was serious.

"You're firing me?? For what?"

"For planting that money on Todd," I said.

"Pfft, prove it!"

"I don't have to. Last week your grandfather installed hidden cameras throughout the place. Should we call him and watch the tape together?"

"Yeah, right. Why didn't he tell me about it?"

"Probably the same reason he didn't trust you to be the manager," I fired back.

I heard a high-pitched, "Oh snap!" come from Freddy's direction.

Chad's face turned shocked, then blank, then pissed.

"Pfft, whatever! This place is a fucking joke anyway. Good luck without me," he laughed as he stood up to leave.

"I think we'll survive," I said.

"With these misfits?" Chad laughed. "Have you taken a good look at your crew? You've got Tinkerbell over here prancing around to his crappy, faggot-ass 80s music. Then there's Mr. 'I'll eat anything for a buck' Phil. You do realize with all your weedwacker, squirrel talk that you're never gonna get laid. EVER!"

Chad then turned his attention to Elise. "Hey, Elise, why don't you do yourself a favor and leave here with me. You don't belong with these losers."

I think he actually assumed that she'd just get up and leave with him. She didn't. Uncomfortable with the situation, she lowered her eyes from Chad's stare.

"Unless you're a loser too?" Chad added.

"Hey! Lay off her, asshole!" Megan interrupted.

Chad looked over at Megan and smiled. "Ahh, which brings me to *Little Miss town slut.*"

"Fuck you!" she yelled.

"Been there done that, remember? And not only do you suck as a waitress, you suck at fucking too! You would think with all your experience you'd be better at it."

Megan's face was red with anger, but more so with embarrassment.

"At least she's not an arrogant douchebag like you!" blurted out Elise.

That's right, quiet, shy Elise said douchebag. Everyone looked over at her in shock. She again lowered her eyes, equally in shock from her outburst.

"Yeah, what she said!" barked Phil.

"I second that," smiled Megan.

Freddy raised his hand and excitedly blurted out, "Samesies."

How does one respond to that? They don't. Chad said nothing more and simply stormed off. As he exited the Lounge, everyone at our table let out a loud cheer. And by everyone, I mean Freddy. Even our waitress seemed happy, and with that, she finally took our drink order.

Megan turned to Elise and grinned, "You don't say much, Elise, but when you do —"

"We have hidden cameras?" interrupted Freddy. "No one told me we had cameras. Are they in the little boys room too? Please tell me they're not in there too?"

"Why? What the hell do you do in there, Freddy?" Megan interrogated.

Freddy covered his mouth in slight embarrassment. "Not *that*, silly goose. I just like my alone time in there. The restroom is not unlike church to me."

"You usually drop deuces in church?" asked Phil. Freddy gave Phil a playful look.

"Relax, Freddy," I said. "There aren't any cameras in the bathroom or otherwise. I had a feeling Chad planted it, so I bluffed."

"Somebody's been watching NYPD Blue," smiled a relieved Freddy.

"Listen, guys, I'm not here to be a hard-ass manager. From what I can tell, you guys do a great job already, and now that Chad is gone, maybe things will run a little more smoothly. I'm not here to bust balls, I'm just trying to collect a paycheck like you, so it'd be easier if we all just worked together."

My pep talks were sounding more and more like Mr. Murphy every day. Everyone nodded in agreement. I could tell, however, that Megan's mind was still on Chad's hurtful words.

"Hey," I yelled over to her, "don't let him get to you, okay? You're a good person and one hell of a waitress."

"You don't think I talk too much to my customers?" she asked.

I shook my head no. "It's how you interact with them that sets you apart from the average waitress." This brought a smile to Megan's face. "But," I continued, "you might not offer so much personal information to them."

"Yeah," she agreed. "I probably shouldn't have told that old couple that I was in a bad mood because I was raggin' it."

We all cringed and laughed in agreement.

"And Freddy," I said, "I love your crappy 80's music. As a matter of fact, you can be in charge of the restaurant's music from now on."

"Shut the crap up!" he said with widened, elated eyes.

As the waitress brought us our drinks, I looked over at Elise and laughed, "Arrogant douchebag, huh?"

She blushed and innocently shrugged.

Megan raised her drink, "A toast, to the arrogant douchebag." Everyone laughed and clinked glasses.

Afterwards, Phil turned to me and whispered, "Do you think he's right? About me never getting laid?"

Usually deadpan and expressionless, Phil actually had a hint of sadness in his voice. I was taken aback. I guess despite his weirdness, I just assumed he had gotten laid… at least once.

"I wouldn't worry about it, Phil," I said. "It'll happen when it's right."

Oh my God, I sounded like his mother or something. Despite the motherly sounding advice, Phil seemed appreciative of it.

"But maybe you should lose some of that weedwacker, squirrel talk. And maybe, just maybe, cut back on the whole eating flies thing."

Phil slapped me on the back and smiled. I actually made Phil smile. Between calling an employee meeting, and my pep talk, and the dramatic firing of Chad, I was on roll tonight. My babbling seemed very limited, and the right words just flowed out perfectly. So much so, that I decided I was going to ask Elise out. Unfortunately, with all the laughing and talking going on at our table, I didn't really get a chance to talk to her.

My chance didn't come until the end of the night. Megan ran into some friends and decided she was going to hang out there longer. Freddy lived around the block so he ended up walking home. And considering that Phil still didn't have a license, he rode his bike home. That just left Elise and myself.

Because the restaurant was directly off the beach, all of the parking spaces were metered (expensively). The only free parking was about a five minute walk up by the ball field. That's where I was parked, and more importantly, it was where Elise was parked too.

Not much was said during our short walk. I used the time

to rehearse the perfect words to ask her out.

"You really didn't have to walk me," she politely said as we approached her blue Honda Accord.

"It's okay. My car is here anyway. It was kinda fun tonight, huh?" I asked.

"Yeah, it was."

"We should do it again sometime. Except maybe next time just you and me?"

How smooth was that? I really was on a roll tonight, or so I thought. A hesitant look came over her face. Was I moving too fast? Her look definitely said I was moving too fast... I think. I panicked and hastily tried to salvage my question. In doing so, I sort of fell back into my babbling thing.

"Not like a *date*, date. More like a non-date, date," I clarified. "We can just hang out and chill. Definitely not a real date though. Not that a real date with you would be bad... because it wouldn't... not at all."

If I ended it there, I might have been semi-okay, but I didn't.

"I just don't want you to think I'm hitting on you. Don't get me wrong, you're definitely hit-onable." A shy smirk crossed her face. She thought I was nuts. "I think you're a really cool chick... woman... girl, whatever."

Her smirk turned into a chuckle, and it wasn't an *aww, you're so adorable* chuckle. It was more like, *this dude is a babbling fool* chuckle.

"I just think it'd be cool if we went out sometime," I

continued. "That way we can get to know each other better. Besides, there are so many questions I wanna ask you."

"Trust me, I'm not that interesting," she said.

"Why would you say that? I already have tons of questions for you."

"Questions, huh?" she smiled as she took her car keys out of her purse. "Like what's my favorite color kind of questions?" she laughed.

"Um, that particular question wasn't really in my head. Besides, I'm thinking it's blue. I notice you always have something blue on."

Again, if I left it at that, I would have been semi-okay, but I didn't.

"And you look great in it too. Not that you don't look great in other colors, because I'm sure you do. It's just, well, blue on you is like, wow. And speaking of wow, you looked super-cute the first time I saw you. Shit, cute isn't a good word, is it? I'm not talking about puppy dogs and teddy bear cute… more like sexy-cute."

Yup, I just called her sexy-cute.

"Oh my God, I'm totally not calling you sexy! I'm not, not calling you sexy either. I guess what I mean is you look nice… really nice."

"Hesitantly, she replied, "Um, thank you, I think."

I just spent forty-two seconds on a complimentary, albeit, run-on sentence, and all she could say was, 'Um, thank you, I think?' This is not how I drew this conversation up. It never is I guess. She unlocked her car door and started to open it.

"Wait. You're leaving? What about my questions?" I asked. "I'm dying to know more about you. The ins and outs of Elise. What makes Elise Carlile tick."

"What makes Elise tick tonight is hitting the sack. I'm exhausted. Guess you'll have to write down your questions for another time," she smiled and climbed into her car. "Goodnight, Josh."

"Goodnight, Elise," I said.

One would think I'd be disheartened by the way this night ended, but the fact that she said 'for another time' gave me hope.

After I watched her taillights fade, I got in my car and headed home. As I drove by the darkened basketball court, I noticed someone shooting hoops. The lights from the surrounding parking lot allowed a little bit of light, but overall the courts were pretty dark.

Actually, this time of night was my favorite time to shoot around. There's something about being alone in the dark, with the sound of the ocean in the distance, shooting hoops. I usually find it's a great way to take out my frustrations of the day.

On closer inspection, I noticed that tonight's sole shooter was Todd. I drove past the court, but for some reason, I found myself circling back around and pulled into the parking lot.

"This is the best time to shoot around," I said as I

approached Todd.

"If you're here to do a strip search, you can turn the fuck around and go home. I didn't take his fuckin' money!"

I rebounded his shot and tossed it back to him.

"I know you didn't. That's why I fired Chad tonight."

Todd's shooting motion came to a halt. "Yeah, right," he said in disbelief.

"It's true. I fired him in front of everyone. It was actually pretty epic."

"You're telling me that you fired the owner's grandson?"

"Yup. Grandson or not, Mr. Murphy hates liars. Besides, I don't think he likes him that much anyway."

I assumed by me telling Todd that I fired Chad, it would be a good bonding moment between us.

"I think Mr. M had it right, Todd. You and I are a lot alike," I pointed out.

"We are nothing alike!" he said as he took another shot.

Maybe our bonding moment would have to wait a bit longer.

"Look, Todd, you might be a prankster, and a wise-ass, and dislike authority figures, but I knew you weren't a thief. I'm not trying to take over your turf, I'm just doing Mr. M a favor this summer."

Without a word, Todd launched and missed an eighteen footer. The ball rolled behind the basket against the guard rail. I walked over, picked it up, and yelled over to Todd, "I'll see you tomorrow, okay?"

"I told you, I quit!" he snapped back.

"That's what they all say," I mumbled as I shot the ball from behind the basket.

To both of our surprise, it went in... nothing but net. You could give me twenty shots and I couldn't do that again. I usually like to save that kind of luck shot for when there are girls around to impress, but the way this night had gone, I'd take it. It was the perfect dramatic exit.

8

"HEAD ON" – Jesus & Mary Chain

The fact that Chad was no longer there, gave the restaurant a much better feel the next day; lighter, a bit more positive. Of course, that didn't stop Megan from worrying about things.

"Have you given any thought how you're gonna replace Todd and Chad?" she asked.

"Chad will be easy," interrupted Phil. "A squirrel on acid could replace him."

Megan and I looked blankly at Phil, but both nodded in agreement.

"Chad was definitely a waste of space," said Megan, "but if it gets busy today, Elise and I are gonna have a tough time keeping up." Megan then looked over at Phil and said, "And without Todd, there's no way Phil can handle the kitchen."

"Eh, don't worry," I said. "Todd will be back, and if he's not, I can help Phil out. After all, I am a legend here."

My joke caused Megan to roll her eyes, and it caused Phil to smile and hit me with a high-five.

"And as far as Chad's replacement is concerned," I said, "I have an idea."

Ironically, my *idea* was about to walk through the front door, or more specifically, bounce through the door. And once again, I know you think I'm just stereotyping, but I swear, Freddy doesn't walk, he bounces. Especially when he's in a good mood (which is always).

Freddy entered wearing a shirt that said, *I wish my life was a John Hughes film.* Don't we all, I thought. He was also wearing his headphones and came in singing Bon Jovi's "You Give Love a Bad Name." When he saw all of us staring at him, he slipped off his headphones and said, "Bonjour, everyone. Or as I like to say, Bon Jovi everyone!"

Freddy didn't even wait for our reaction to his lame joke. He simply put his music back on and danced his way into the kitchen. In my head, I began a countdown. *5...4...3...2...* Just as I hit 1, Freddy busted back into the dining room in a panic.

"Why is there a young teenage boy doing *my* dishes?" Freddy asked, almost shaking.

"Oh, that's my neighbor's kid, Aaron. He's our new

dishwasher," I announced.

Freddy immediately fell to his knees and put his head in his hands and dramatically said, "You're firing me too? This can't be happening. Did you know about this?" he looked over at Phil and Megan, who were equally surprised at the new dishwasher. "This must be how David Lee Roth felt when they booted him from Van Halen." Freddy was nearly in tears.

"Settle down, David Lee," I laughed. "You're not getting fired. You're getting promoted… to waiter."

Freddy's fake tears and whining stopped immediately as he muttered, "I am?"

"He is?" chimed in Megan and Phil.

"Sure, why not?" I said. "You're a people person. You're animated, you're enthusiastic… and did I mention animated? Besides, I think your skills are going to waste as a dishwasher."

"They are?" he asked as he got off his knees and stood up. "I mean, yeah, they are!" He proudly straightened his posture. "I always wanted to be a waiter. Thank you, thank you, thank you. I'd give you a big hug right now, Joshua, but that's probably not something a new waiter should be doing with his boss, huh? I'm a waiter, I'm a waiter!" he repeated as he spun his way back into the kitchen.

"You totally just created a monster," Megan said.

"A gay monster at that," added Phil.

***

The lunch rush was busier than normal, but Megan, Elise, and Freddy handled it perfectly. Freddy was a natural. Thirty-one. Thirty-one was the number of times Freddy thanked me for his promotion.

I probably shouldn't admit this, but it was fun being thrown back into the kitchen during a big rush. Despite being an odd duck, Phil knew how to bang out the orders. Our only setback was when Phil's button popped off his pants. But before they even had the chance to fall to his ankles, he not only stapled them shut, but he had crafted a duct tape belt. MacGyver would be proud.

After the lunch rush was over, I headed into the dining room to check on things. I wasn't in there a second when you know who walked through the front door. Todd.

I smiled and thought, *better late than never*. Megan and Elise also were smiling. Freddy's reaction was a little bit more... Freddy-esque.

"Toddles! You're back! Do I look any different?" Freddy slowly turned around modeling his new waiter apron and his order pad. Before Todd could reply, Freddy gave him a huge hug. "Oh Toddles, we missed you so much."

Todd broke free of Freddy's hug and said, "You just saw me last night, ya idiot!"

His words went in one ear and out the other as Freddy continued looking him over. "You look relaxed. I can see your time off was good for you."

Todd knew his reply was pointless, so he just shook his head and walked towards the kitchen. I threw him a welcoming smile, but as expected, it wasn't reciprocated. Either way, we were all glad he was back.

Considering I was in the kitchen cooking the first half of the day, I didn't really get a chance to talk to Elise, but that didn't mean I wasn't checking her out. She had her blue-rimmed glasses on and her hair was in short, tight pigtails. It wasn't until she walked by carrying a large order that I said something.

I gave her a subtle, yet cool nod and said, "Diggin' the glasses… and the tails."

She gave me her typical shy, embarrassed Elise smile and continued by me.

"Oh God, just ask her out already."

I turned around to see Megan standing there.

Before I could respond to Megan, I noticed her eyes widen as she looked over my shoulder. Curiously, I turned back around to see Elise awkwardly attempting to balance all the plates as she neared the table. My mind flashed back to the first time I saw her on the beach when she fell and launched the lotion onto Frenchy. I also remembered her self-proclamation as the world's biggest klutz. She was about to reinforce those words. Bigtime.

I'm not quite sure how she did it, but she clumsily tripped over her own feet which caused the plates to come crashing down onto the floor. Well, not all of them hit the floor. The plate of pasta with meatballs flew towards a table of four J-Crew-looking frat boys. I shit you not, the plate landed upside down directly on one guy's crotch.

"Oh my God," laughed Megan. "This chick is a walking disaster."

"Yeah," I smiled, "isn't she great?"

The shock and horror on Elise's face was priceless. I mean, I totally felt bad for the poor girl, but what we just witnessed was comic gold! The only thing funnier was what ensued next. The frat dude stared down at the plateful of pasta on his crotch, and with a cocky and perverted smirk, he raised his crotch up towards Elise.

"I tell you what, sweetheart, I'll let you wipe it up. Be gentle," he said as his frat buddies cracked up laughing.

Before Elise could utter a word, the kitchen door burst open, and almost magically, Freddy appeared at the table with a cloth in hand.

"Let me get that for you," Freddy said as he removed the plate and began sensually wiping the guy's crotch area.

The whole restaurant watched in awe and obvious amusement. I even noticed Todd peer out of the kitchen with a smile on his face. The frat dude quickly shut his legs and pushed Freddy's hand away.

"Hey! Enough! I can get it myself," the frat dude yelled.

"Sorry," offered Freddy, "I was just trying to clean up all the meatballs."

"Those weren't meatballs, ya fag!"

And just like that, the hilarious moment turned sour. I was forced to put on my manager's hat and step in. I apologized for the incident, refunded them their money, and politely asked them to leave. I also had to tell Freddy that it'd be a good idea to let customers wipe their own crotches in the future.

Considering that Elise was still quite embarrassed, I figured she needed a famous Josh pep talk, but Megan beat me to it. She followed Elise into the back, and when they returned, they were both smiling and laughing. I really did have a good crew; dysfunctional and bat-shit-crazy, but a good crew. The bat-shit-crazy (& disgusting) portion of that statement would be on full display around closing time that night.

9

"BIGMOUTH STRIKES AGAIN" – The Smiths

When I finished balancing the registers, I exited the office and walked in on another famous and disgusting dare. Todd had just finished sweeping the kitchen floor. I'm not sure if you've ever seen a restaurant's floor at the end of the night, but it usually consists of dirt, food, grime, hairballs, and other unidentified shit. I watched as Todd stared at the dustpan full of said concoction.

"Hey Phil," yelled Todd, "eight bucks if you eat two giant spoonfuls of this."

Phil didn't answer right away, instead, carefully pondered. Even Phil had a line he wouldn't cross, right? Wrong.

"Put it on a hamburger bun, give me a chaser of water,

and I'll eat the whole dustpan for fourteen bucks."

I had never ever seen negotiating like this. It was so matter of fact, so... fucking disgusting.

Todd thought about Phil's counter offer then raised it to another level.

"I'll make it nineteen bucks, but instead of water as a chaser, you use clam juice."

"Deal!" Phil blurted out way too quickly and way too eagerly.

Part of me knew I needed to put a stop to this, but the other part of me wanted to see if Phil would actually do it. The latter part of me won out. The next thing I knew, the whole crew was gathered around Phil. Todd slowly emptied the dustpan between a hamburger bun. He then grabbed a gallon of clams and poured its juice into a cup. He slid the dirtburger and clam juice in front of Phil. Without hesitation, Phil took a giant bite and proceeded to chase it down with clam juice.

"Oh God, oh God, dry heaves," Freddy announced as he covered his mouth gagging. He then rushed out of the kitchen towards the bathroom.

Phil proudly finished his dustpan sandwich, pounded down his clam juice, and reached his hand out to Todd. "Nineteen bucks!" Phil said.

Todd smiled and handed Phil a twenty and motioned for him to keep the change. And that, my friends, was only day three of work.

The night actually ended on a much higher note than Phil's grotesque eating exhibition. There were only two private, non-metered parking spaces behind the restaurant. Mr. Murphy had one, and he originally offered me the other. But as soon as I found out Elise parked down the street at the ball field, I gladly gave the space to Megan. I quickly locked up the restaurant and rushed ahead to catch up with Elise.

"Hey, I'll walk you to your car," I said.

"You really don't…"

"Have to?" I finished her sentence. "I know, but I want to. Besides, I'm parked in the ball field too."

I then smoothly moved her from the outside of the sidewalk to the inside. She curiously gazed at me.

"Chivalry," I shrugged. "The man is supposed to walk closest to the traffic. It's an unwritten rule. Actually, it might be a written rule. I'm not really sure."

This caused her to give me a look. I can't really explain the look, but it was one I'd get a lot that summer from her. Her look kind of said, *You're a total dork… but a sweet and kind dork.*

"This little walk will give me a chance to ask you some of my questions on my list," I said.

"Questions? List?" she asked.

"Yeah, you remember? The whole what makes Elise tick thing? You told me to write down my questions for another time. Remember?"

"I was kidding," she laughed.

"Oh," my voice lowered, "I thought you were serious, so I wrote all fifty-seven of them down."

Her eyes widened. "Oh my God! I'm totally not that interesting. Especially for... wait, did you say fifty-seven questions?"

"Um, yeah," I nodded. "Fifty-six was too few and fifty-eight woulda been an overkill."

And there was that look again. Although this time it was less of the *sweet and kind* and more of the *dork*.

"You really didn't make a list, did you?" she asked.

I reached in my pocket and pulled out a crisply folded paper and showed it to her.

She smiled and shook her head. "Oh man. You're too much. But like I said, I'm totally not interesting enough for fifty-seven questions."

"We'll see," I smiled undeterred. "Okay, let's start with some basics. Favorite drink?"

I could tell she was still in disbelief about my list, but she smiled and answered, "Diet Coke. But from the can. It tastes better from the can."

"Diet Coke from the can. Nice! See," I said, "isn't this fun?"

"Yeah, a blast," she joked.

"Ok, next question: Favorite movie?"

Elise thought for a second then smirked. "I'm not sure about a favorite movie, but I'll tell you my favorite type of movie. It's gonna shock you though. They're kind of a guilty pleasure of mine."

"Holy crap," I said, "you like porn, too?"

"Eww, no! I was talking about Kung Fu movies."

I started laughing until I realized she was serious.

"Like Bruce Lee type stuff?" I asked.

She smiled and nodded. "The cheesier the better. You know, the kind of movie where the voices don't match up with their mouths, and the sound effects are way over the top? Aren't those great?"

"You're totally serious, aren't you?" I said.

What happened next not only cracked me up but it cemented my infatuation with her. She began talking as if she was in one of those movies - her mouth and voice not syncing up at all.

"Of course I'm serious. And if you have a problem with that, maybe you can take it up with the Master of the Flying Guillotine?" She finished her badly dubbed dialogue with some sort of Kung Fu moves. The normally shy and quiet Elise had once again blown my mind.

All I could muster was, "The Master of the Flying Guillotine?"

"Uh yeah. It's a classic."

I was left speechless by her utter cuteness. When we finally reached her car, I joked, "Can you imagine if they made Kung Fu pornos?"

I probably should have stayed speechless.

"You're ridiculous," she said shaking her head.

"Pfft, you're ridiculous. Kung Fu movies? Flying guillotines? I thought for sure you'd go with the typical chick-flick movies like 'When Harry Met Sally' type stuff."

"Nah. I'm not really a fan of chick-flicks. 'When Harry Met Sally' was entertaining and all, but I just don't buy into that kind of crap."

"That kind of crap?" I asked.

"Yeah, the whole true love, soulmate, happily ever after stuff."

"Ah, that kind of crap," I smirked. "I didn't take you for a pessimist."

Sadly, Elise shrugged. I suppose that should have forewarned me to not ask those type of questions, but I went there anyway. I opened my list back up.

"That's a perfect lead in for my next two questions. How long was your longest relationship?"

"Not very," she responded. I gave her a *could you be more specific?* motion. She sighed then answered, "Longer than they shoulda been. How about we just leave it at that?"

I should have left it at that, but I moved onto an even more uncomfortable question.

"Next question: Ever been in love?"

Elise became quiet. Uncomfortably quiet. Her demeanor — sadder. I immediately regretted pushing the topic, but it was too late.

She fumbled with her keys and politely said, "I should probably get going. I'm going out with Nikki later. Thanks again for the walk. Night."

With that, she got into her car. I wanted to apologize, but chose instead to just say, "Goodnight Elise." I watched her taillights fade then I got into my car. I sat there, gave myself a good yelling at, then drove home.

10

"INBETWEEN DAYS" – The Cure

The next couple of shifts were boring and uneventful. The boring part was mostly due to Elise having two days off. It's amazing how less motivated I was coming to work knowing she wasn't going to be there. I suppose it wasn't totally boring at the restaurant. Between listening to Megan tell her life story to her customers, and Freddy acting out his stories, I was pretty entertained.

I was even warming up and entertained by Phil's wry and twisted sense of humor. Todd and I still weren't buddy-buddy, but things were better, more civil. We even shared a laugh or three at Freddy being Freddy.

For instance, like the time I was on the phone placing an

order and Freddy came skipping in singing the classic 80's cheerleader anthem, "Hey Mickey." He stopped directly in front of Todd and did his best cheerleader movements as he sang.

"Alright! Enough of that crap, Freddy!" Todd said annoyed.

Freddy smiled and handed Todd an order slip then cheered his way back into the dining room. I watched Todd start to cook the order and then it happened; the classic case of stupid-song-stuck-in-your-head. The next thing I knew, Todd was cooking while whistling the "Hey Mickey" tune.

When he finally realized what he was doing, he slowly looked around to see if anyone had heard. It was too late, for there, at the kitchen door, stood Freddy, grinning widely.

"Not a fuckin' word," warned Todd.

"Why Toddles, I think I'm rubbing off on you," Freddy giggled.

"Trust me, you're not rubbing anything on me!"

Freddy giggled again. "Ohh, youuu."

***

The day went from funny to absurd. Ridiculously absurd. As in, Geoff Part II. As soon as he walked in the door, I hit him with, "Hey Geoff, burn any places down lately?"

Geoff snapped back with, "No. I don't talk like that anymore."

"Yeah, Josh," Megan smiled, "Geoff is a changed man since last week."

I noticed Geoff clutching his stomach in discomfort.

"What's wrong with your stomach?" I asked.

"Probably too many hot dog and garlic quesadillas," Megan joked.

Geoff shook his head no and uttered, "No. Too much chocolate."

Before he even got the word chocolate out, Freddy magically appeared by Geoff's side.

"Chocolate? Did I hear you say chocolate? I love chocolate. Any left?" Freddy eagerly asked.

Geoff reached into his pocket and pulled out a box of Ex-Lax. Freddy's excitement went from a *ten* to a *one*.

"Oh, Geoffy," Freddy disappointedly said, "that is sooo not chocolate."

"Are you joking or serious?" Geoff asked sluggishly.

"Ass chocolate," laughed Megan.

"Da ha ha ha, ass chocolate," laughed Geoff.

Not wanting to deal with this, I grabbed the Ex-Lax and threw it away on my way into the back office. I barely sat down, when there was a quiet knock on my door. It was Elise. On her day off. Giving me puppy-dog eyes.

"Oh no," I sighed. "Please don't tell me you're quitting?"

"No, I'm not quitting," she smiled. "But I was kind of wondering if there was any way I could get a few more days off this week. Totally last minute plans, but Nikki and I were invited up to Montreal with some friends tomorrow." She paused a second then continued, "But I totally understand if you can't..."

"It's fine," I said. "We'll be all set."

"Really?" she smiled. "Thanks! I owe you one. I promise I'll work extra shifts when I get back."

"Yeah, yeah, yeah," I said.

Before she walked off, I felt the need to apologize to her.

"Hey, I'm sorry if I got too personal with some of my questions the other night."

"It's okay," she shrugged. "I'm just not a big fan of talking about my past relationships, that's all."

"Understood," I nodded. On her way off, I blurted out, "What about bonfires? Are you a big fan of bonfires? Some of my friends are having one tonight up by the lighthouse. I was sorta wondering if you maybe wanna go with me? You know, a non-date, date sorta thing?"

"Actually, I can't. Freddy invited me to go watch him do karaoke. I guess his friends are all working late and he didn't want to go alone. It should quite entertaining."

"To say the least," I said. "Rain check?"

A polite, yet hesitant smile formed on her lips, and as she turned to go she merely said, "Thanks again for the time off."

Did she not understand that the *rain check question* was a yes or no question? Most people would have chalked up her non-response as a big, fat no, but I'm not most people. I still held out hope. I didn't get a chance to think too heavily on it, as

Todd's voice entered the office.

"Ahh, giving Elise extra time off and buttering her up with silly questions about herself, huh? I'll give you credit, you're definitely pulling out all the stops to get into her pants."

"What?" I said shocked. "That's not what I'm doing."

"Hey, don't worry, bossman, your plan is safe with me."

Before I could defend myself, Todd had disappeared into the kitchen, chuckling. Just when I thought Todd and I had an understanding, he went and basically accused me of being like Chad. Like fuckin' Chad! I rushed into the kitchen to set the record straight, but before I could, I was approached by Megan.

"You might wanna come into the dining room," she said. "I think we have a code red."

My first thought was maybe Elise had another tripping incident on her way out, or maybe Freddy was attempting to inappropriately grope another customer. Defending myself to Todd would have to wait.

Surprisingly, Elise was upright and accident free, and Freddy's hands were by his side. Megan pointed to the bathrooms in the back. There was a line of three guys impatiently waiting for the men's room. The first guy gave the door a loud rap then glared over at me.

"What seems to be the problem?" I asked.

"Some idiot has been in there for a half an hour now and every time I knock, he just laughs this weird laugh."

I had my suspicions, so I gave the door a quick knock.

"Da ha ha ha." came from inside.

Suspicions confirmed.

"Open the door, Geoff," I barked.

"Da ha ha ha, ass chocolate," laughed Geoff.

"Oh boy." I sighed to Megan. "Please tell me we have a key for this door?" Slowly, she shook her head no. "Oh boy," I repeated. "I guess we're gonna have to pick the lock."

The next thing I knew, Phil was standing next to me, digging into his fanny pack. What is it with my employees magically appearing? Among random trinkets and his trusty roll of duct tape, Phil pulled out a paper clip and proceeded to pick the lock. Once the lock was picked, Phil gave me a salute and marched back into the kitchen.

I placed my hand on the knob and hesitantly turned it. I had only opened it a quarter of the way, when I felt my jaw drop to the floor in awe and disgust... utter, utter disgust.

"Ohh, Geoff. What did you do?" I said, covering my nose and mouth. The smell alone sent the three guys in line back to their seats and then out the front door. In the corner of the small bathroom, crouched Geoff... naked... covering up his privates... and laughing.

"Da ha ha ha."

"This is NOT funny, Geoff!" I scolded.

"Are you joking or serious?" he predictably said.

I didn't even answer him. I was too busy staring at the shit-smeared walls. His clothes, along with a whole roll of toilet paper, were strewn across the floor.

"More like a code brown than a code red, huh?" laughed Megan from behind me.

I didn't share in the humor. Situations like this were definitely not in the job description. At this point, I had no choice but to call the police. No, not to arrest Geoff (Apparently it's not a crime to shit yourself in a public place). But, considering I had a naked man in the bathroom, and considering his clothes were way too soiled to put back on, I had to do something.

Luckily, I was friends with one of the summer beach cops, so I had him come and assist me with my situation. He covered Geoff with a blanket and escorted him out the back door and to his house. Needless to say, my cop friend never let me forget just how much I owed him.

Getting Geoff out of the bathroom was only phase one. Phase two was the clean-up. Before I could return to the scene of the crime, Megan and Elise approached me.

"Is it me or did Geoff have a shit-eating grin on his face," joked Megan.

Elise nodded and shrugged, "Oh well, shit happens."

"You girls won't be laughing if you're the ones cleaning the bathroom," I warned.

"Oh, fuck no!" Megan said. "Our asses will quit before that'll happen. And don't even think about Freddy. He's in the girl's room right now, dry heaving."

"Well I'm not gonna do it," I said. "I guess we're gonna have to hire a professional cleaning service."

"I'll do it." And there, magically appearing by my side, was Phil.

"Really?" we all asked.

"Sure," he shrugged. "How much is it worth to you?" he smiled.

"I'll give you twenty," I said turning towards the girls.

"I'll put in another twenty," Megan said.

"Samesies," called Freddy's voice from the ladies room.

"Sixty bucks?" exclaimed Phil. "I would have done it for $23.85. Suckers!" he said as he headed off for cleaning supplies.

Megan said what we all were thinking, "Reason 72 why he'll never get laid." We all nodded.

Armed with a mop and an arsenal of cleaning products, Phil returned. He opened the bathroom door and took it all in. He seemed unaffected by the pure nastiness of it. Actually, he seemed... intrigued.

"It's as if he was a shit artist," he mumbled to himself. "A Picasso of shit, if you will, and the walls are his canvas." Phil paused, then turned his head towards the ceiling. "Wow! How did he get some way up there?" He then contorted his own ass upwards, as if to recreate the scene.

Freddy finally exited the ladies room, but as soon as he saw and smelled the men's room, he covered his mouth and sprinted back into the bathroom, dry heaving the whole way.

With all the commotion regarding the *shit incident*, I didn't get a chance to clear up the Elise misunderstanding with

Todd. He slipped out before I could say something. I hated being compared to guys like Chad.

11

"END OF THE WORLD" - REM

The bonfire was at our friend Evan's house; his parent's summer house. Most of the people here tonight, including Evan, were just summer friends. I don't mean that in a bad way, it was just the facts. They were here from Memorial Day to Labor Day, then headed back to college or wherever they were from. Ninety percent of the time, we wouldn't see or hear from them again until the following summer. 'Good-time friends' is probably the best way to put it.

By now, most of us were in our mid-twenties, so a lot of them had real jobs elsewhere and were only able to come to Maine on weekends. Some of them, like Pete, were engaged. A couple of them were not only married already, but had kids.

I was greeted by Scott, who handed me a beer.

"Thanks," I said. "Where's your new woman?"

Scott pointed over to a group of people by the fire and said, "She's listening to one of Doug's stories."

"Oh boy," I said. "He's storytelling already, huh?"

I have to admit, Doug's party stories were quite entertaining to say the least. Next, I was approached by a couple of summer girls, Sara Beth and Brianna. Like most people here, I hadn't seen them since last year. They looked the same — tanned and buzzed.

"Oh my God, is it true about the Geoff shit story?" asked Sara Beth.

"How'd you hear about that already?" I asked.

They pointed over to Jeff, the summer cop who assisted me earlier with Geoff.

"Ahh," I smiled. "Yeah, it's true."

"Da ha ha ha," laughed both girls.

Just then, a loud and slightly drunk voice hit me from behind.

"Heyyy! It's DJ Melancholy!"

I turned to see two of my other summer friends, Mike and Andy. These two are the quintessential beach dudes. They spent their summers tanning, surfing, and partying - not always in that order. They were also known for their late night streaking. At one party a few summers ago, they streaked the entire Long Sands beach. Needless to say, there were several couples out for a late night romantic walk who got more than they bargained for.

Supposedly, back in '91, they wore Nixon and Reagan masks and streaked through the Fun-O-Rama. They got the mask idea from that summer's big movie, "Point Break". They also strategically 'attached' tube socks on their peckers.

Although this story has never really been confirmed by anyone other than Mike and Andy, its legend grows more each summer. One version I heard actually had them stopping at the foosball table for a quick shot or two before bolting out the back door and disappearing into the night.

With regards to why they called me DJ Melancholy: Like I mentioned earlier, the last five summers I DJ'd at a club called Goodnight Ogunquit. The DJ booth was about ten feet above the dance floor and you needed to climb a wooden ladder to get up into it. The lighting in the booth was at a bare minimum; mostly just the two mini lamps over the turntables. I spent much of the time with my headphones on and looking down at the turntables and mixing board. From the crowd's perspective, it looked like the dark silhouette of my head was hung in constant sadness. This was enhanced when I turned on the fog machines and played some Cure. Hence the name, DJ Melancholy.

Seeing Mike, Andy, and the rest of the summer crew really made me miss spinning records at the club. Sure, there were other clubs in the area that I could have DJ'd for, but it wouldn't have been the same. One of the things I loved about my Sunday night at the club was I could play any type of music and the dance floor would still fill up. I didn't have to stick to a specific genre all night like a lot of other clubs. The crowds were so fun and diverse that I could play blocks of everything.

I could go from Naughty By Nature and the Beastie Boys to Depeche Mode and the Smiths, and then I could slide into "Stayin' Alive" by the Bee Gees. From classic 80's to techno and even some reggae – I played it all. And depending on my mood, I would end each night with either "Pictures Of You" by The Cure or "It's The End Of The World As We Know It(And I Feel Fine)".

With that much variety, I never ever got bored. Don't get me wrong, there were certain songs I was forced to play every week that I hated. Take for instance, Robyn Kerrigan. She was a lifeguard over in Ogunquit Beach. Every week, she and her (drunk) friends would request the "Electric Boogie" – otherwise known as the Electric Slide.

Every week I'd play it for them; partly because I was a very accommodating DJ, but mostly because they were fuckin' cute as hell. There were nights when the words "Boogie woogie, woogie" haunted me in my sleep. The one saving grace with that stupid song was watching a dancefloor full of drunk people trying to do the dance.

Another song I was 'forced' to play was "December 1963(Oh, What A Night)" by the Four Seasons. This idiotic song was religiously requested by Heather Strong and her (drunk) friends – AKA 'The Marshwood girls'. This chick-crew was from a couple towns over in Eliot, Maine.

I hated that song, but I played it for them every week because I was a nice guy... and yes, they may or may not have been fuckin' cute as well.

I joined Scott and Pete over by the fire just in time to catch the end of one of Doug's stories. Michelle was off mingling and showing off her ring. Over the next hour, I drank a little and reminisced a lot.

Doug took a break from storytelling and joined Frank Clines who was sitting playing guitar. It wasn't a party until Frank started playing his guitar. And it certainly wasn't a party until Doug or myself joined him on vocals. But seeing as I was far from drunk, I let Doug go solo. He always started off with the real lyrics but quickly began to ad-lib, and before you knew it, he had created an original Doug song. No matter what song it was, he always worked in the word China. Why? Because he could rhyme it with vagina. 'Nuff said.

It was great seeing the whole summer crew again, but most of the night, my mind was still on Elise. Yup, my summer had just started and I already had an infatuation. So much, in fact, I decided to bail early and head over to where Freddy was doing Karaoke.

Little did I know, as I said my goodbyes and left, this would be the last time our core summer crew would be at the same party together. Despite my Elise infatuation, if I would have known this would be our final party all together, I never would have left early. I would have stayed all night... enjoyed it more... appreciated it more. But like most moments in life, there's no forewarning. You just never know when a moment will be the last.

12

"TAILLIGHTS FADE" – Buffalo Tom

The karaoke night Elise referred to was being held in the lounge of the Union Bluff Hotel. The Bluff was perched behind Fun-O-Rama arcade on the rocky cove overlooking Short Sands Beach. When I entered the dimly lit lounge, Freddy was already on stage belting out, "Somebody to Love" by Queen. Freddy owned the stage, and it was obvious that the stage is where he belonged. As he did his best Freddy Mercury imitation, I spotted Elise sitting in the front row. I decided to hang back until Freddy finished his song.

What happened next could only be described as embarrassingly awesome! Towards the end of the song, Freddy reached out his hand for Elise to join him on stage.

And in true 'shy Elise' fashion, she vehemently shook her head no. The small crowd clapped and yelled out for her to do it. Finally, Elise actually gave in and reluctantly joined Freddy on the tiny make-shift stage.

I'm still not sure exactly what she tripped on, but the next thing I knew, she did a major face plant onto the stage. The crowd cringed in unison. Despite the smile on my face, I felt horribly for Elise. I really did. Being the consummate performer, Freddy didn't miss a beat. He smiled and continued to sing, all the while helping Elise to her feet. Her face was bright red.

When Freddy got to the repetitive "Find me somebody to love" part, he alternated the mic between he and Elise. On her first go around, she was unsure and off pitch, but on her second go around she sounded pretty good actually. So good in fact, Freddy motioned to her to sing the pinnacle part of the song. And sing she did. With confidence, grace, and a pitch perfect tone, Elise absolutely nailed the ending.

When the song was over, the small crowd sat in silence for a few seconds before erupting in loud applause. Freddy covered his mouth in shock and fell to his knees, giving Elise the 'I'm not worthy' bow. He then hugged her and guided her (safely) to their table.

"Holy shitballs!" he exclaimed. "That was africkinmazing!"

"It sure was," I said as I approached their table.

"Joshua? What are you doing here?" he asked.

"Apparently, I'm watching Elise upstage the great

Freddy."

"I know, right?" he giggled. "Who would have thought Miss Thang over here can belt it like Aretha?" Freddy motioned for me to have a seat with them.

"Keep Elise company, Joshua, I have to go use the little boy's room. In all that excitement, I may or may not have peed myself a little."

As he headed off, Elise and I shook our heads at Freddy being Freddy.

"So what happened to your bonfire?" she asked.

"It was okay, but let's just say I'm not a big fan of realizing that most my friends are either married or engaged to be married... and/or have kids already."

"Ahh, feeling old and single, huh?" she said.

"Yeah, something like that."

"So you decided to come hang out with me and Freddy in hopes of feeling young again. Take a drink from our fountains' of youth, if you will." Immediately, she caught herself. "Whoa! That totally sounded perverted, didn't it?"

I smiled and made the 'little bit' gesture with my fingers. It was nice being on the other side of an embarrassing comment.

After Freddy finished talking with a friend in the back, he came over and said, "So, here's the deal, the rest of my friends are out of work and they want me to meet them up in Ogunquit at the Fuzzy Banana Bar & Grill. You two are welcome to join us."

"Ah yes," I smirked, "The Fuzzy Banana."

"Joshua! Don't tell me you're a homophobe?"

"Freddy, my friend, I'm totally not a homophobe," I smiled. "I just make it a rule not to go to bars named after fruit... hairy or otherwise."

"I think I'll pass too," Elise laughed.

With a disappointed smirk, Freddy looked at us and said, "Fine, suit yourself." He then gave Elise a big hug and kiss on the cheek. "You were amazing tonight! Have fun in Montreal."

"Thanks," she replied.

Freddy then turned to me with arms opened wide. I was tempted to let him have his moment, but instead, I reached out my hand for a shake. He rolled his eyes (dramatically) and shook my hand.

I love Freddy, but him leaving Elise and me alone couldn't have been planned any better. We could sit, have a couple of drinks, and finally get a chance to get to know each other. Her first sentence after Freddy left quickly put an end to that theory.

"Well, I should probably head out too," she said. "Nikki went out tonight with some random guy she met on the beach today. I'm dying to hear how it turned out."

"If it turns out anywhere near good, you do realize she won't be home for another few hours, if at all," I pointed out.

"I know, I know," she said, "but if it doesn't go well, I want to be there for her."

"Do you need a ride?" I asked.

"Nah," she said. "I'm parked down the road in the beach parking lot."

"I'll walk you to your car. And yes, I know I don't have to. I want to."

She rolled her eyes and joked, "If you insist."

As we headed up the sidewalk, I couldn't resist, "Oh, by the way, that was a stellar face plant on stage tonight. Very rock-n-roll of you."

"Oh God." She covered her face. "You saw that? I told you, I'm the clumsiest girl in the world."

"Yeah, but your singing more than made up for it. Where in the world did you learn how to sing like that?"

"Eh, it's kind of an embarrassing hidden talent," she said.

I smiled widely, "Number nineteen!"

"Huh?" She curiously questioned.

"I believe number nineteen on my questions' list is tell me an Elise hidden talent that would shock me."

"Number nineteen?" she said incredulously. "Yeah, right."

Her skeptical tone was squashed when I pulled out my list and showed her number nineteen. Quite bemused, she shook her head at me while I awaited an answer.

"Fine," she sighed. "I used to sing in a choir."

"Like for school assemblies?" I asked.

"No," she laughed. "That would be the chorus. I sang in the choir... as in church. It was when I was young, and I only did it because my parents forced me. The choir actually led by a monk."

"A monk? So you guys did chanting and shit?"

"No," she quickly answered. "As in church-type songs. It's not like I do it anymore," she clarified.

"Nothing to be embarrassed about," I assured. "I never went to church myself, but I heard it's nice. Pretty windows and shit."

"You're such a dork," she laughed.

"I'm the dork? You're the one busting out hymns with monks," I said loud enough for the couple walking by us to hear.

"Shhh," she said. "Not many people know that about me. So keep it on the DL, okay?"

"Ahh, I'll keep it on the double DL, the DDL."

"You really are a dork," she smiled as we entered the beach parking lot. I knew my time was limited, so I made my move.

"So, I was thinking, when you get back from your Montreal trip, we should go out."

The hesitation in her eyes was immediate, and I knew an avalanche of emotion was about to come crashing down on me.

"Umm... I don't know," she slowly began. "You are my boss and all, and I don't want people thinking things. Besides, I'm only here for the summer, and I'm not really looking for anything serious. We can still talk and hang out at work though."

I was just crushed by the *let's just be friends* rock. I've never been good at hiding my emotions, so my giant feeling of disappointment was easily detected by her. I could tell she felt bad about bursting my bubble, and then, of course, I felt bad about her feeling bad.

"I tell you what, if it'll cheer you up, you can ask me another one of your questions," she said sweetly.

I was still reeling from rejection and was completely disenchanted at the thought of asking her more of my questions.

"Come on," she smiled, "you know you want to. How about question number twenty-six?"

Okay, maybe I wasn't completely disenchanted. I pulled out my trusty list and read aloud, "Number twenty-six – What was your best day ever and what was your worst?"

"Wow. That was number twenty-six, huh?" she asked. I nodded. "Hmmm, is it bad that nothing is coming to mind for my best day ever?" I shot her a look. "I swear I'm not trying to avoid answering, but nothing is standing out as my best day ever. I've had a lot of fun days and really good days, but best day ever??"

"Fine," I relented. "Worst day ever?"

Her smile faded, and the usual sparkle in her eyes disappeared and turned to sadness.

"Worst day ever was when my grandfather died."

"I'm sorry, Elise. Were you two close?"

"Very. It's been awhile, but for one or two weeks in the

summer, I'd come out here to visit them at their cottage. Some of my favorite memories were with my grandparents here at the beach."

Seeing the sadness in her eyes, I immediately regretted asking the question. Before I could apologize, she said, "Thanks again for giving me the weekend off and for walking me to my car." She unlocked her door and got in. "Night, Josh."

"Goodnight, Elise," was all I could say as I once again stood there and watched her taillights fade.

13

"WHERE IS MY MIND" – The Pixies

The next day I noticed Todd by himself in the kitchen, and I thought about clearing the air regarding his assumptions of my Elise intentions. My hesitation cost me; Phil entered the kitchen and Todd motioned him over. Apparently Todd just finished making his secret clam chowder recipe. He wanted Phil to sample it, which in itself was quite strange.

"Do you really want the guy who eats flies and dustpan sandwiches to be the judge of that?" I joked.

Phil smiled at my statement. Todd did not. We both took a spoonful and sampled.

"Wow, that's really good, Todd," I said.

Todd wasn't impressed by my compliment. He was more

concerned with what Phil thought. Phil was slow and deliberate with his bite. Finally, after he swallowed, he looked at Todd and said, "It's good, but… but it's missing something. I don't know what, but something."

Todd tasted it himself then nodded in agreement. It was obvious that my opinion didn't matter. And it was also obvious that I wasn't going to get a chance to talk one on one with Todd. So I changed the subject.

"I'm placing an order in a bit. Is there anything you guys need?' I asked.

Without hesitation, Phil blurted out, "I could use a blind, blonde nymphomaniac."

I suppose I should have been happy he didn't include any squirrels or weedwackers, but still… I had no clue what to do or say in response. Luckily, we were interrupted by Freddy, dancing his way into the kitchen singing Prince's "Raspberry Beret."

"Oh. My. God, people," he dramatically announced, "you should see the hottie at table three! And not only is he hot, but he was totally flirting with me."

"How do you know he's gay?" asked Phil.

"Because they can smell their own kind," joked Todd.

Freddy gave Todd a playful glare and said, "Ohhh youuuu." He then grabbed the plate of food and sang his way back into the dining room.

Our curiosity got the best of us as we all went to the dining room door and eavesdropped on Freddy and the 'hottie' at table three. He looked to be in his early twenties. He had well-coiffed jet black hair, designer shorts, and a tight vintage Queen concert tee. Freddy was completely smitten with the dude. I had to laugh to myself. The look he had on his face was probably the same one I had when I saw Elise for the first time.

I think we all know by now, if I was in a situation like this, I would have babbled. Freddy, on the other hand, was more of a tongue-tied conversationalist.

"By the way, this is like my favorite sandwich here," Freddy said, placing the plate in front of the guy.

"Well, it must be good then," the guy answered. "I bet you have great taste."

"Thanks," glowed Freddy, "I bet you taste great too." Freddy quickly caught himself and covered his mouth. "Oops! I mean, I bet you have great taste, too," Freddy said pointing to the guy's shirt. "I totally heart Queen."

"Freddy Mercury is God," smiled the guy.

"I know, right? Ironically, my name is Freddy too. All my friends call me Merc," he giggled.

"No one calls you that," mumbled Megan as she walked by. The guy smiled as Freddy shot her an evil glare.

"My friends call me Steve," he said reaching his hand out to Freddy. They both glowed and shook hands.

That whole 'connection at first meeting' thing rarely ever happened like that for me. I admit it, I was jealous. My jealousy was short-lived when I heard Phil's comment from behind me.

"Oh man! I can't believe he's showing his face here again."

I looked over to the front door and saw Geoff entering.

"Where's Josh?" he asked Megan.

"He got fired," she answered.

"Really?" he said shocked. "Are you joking or serious?"

"I'm serious. He tried to burn this place down."

"Really?" Geoff's shock turned into a smile. "Da ha ha ha," he laughed.

Megan just shook her head and warned, "You better not have eaten any more ass chocolate today, Geoff."

"Da ha ha ha... ass chocolate."

"I'm serious, Geoff! What you did the other day was the most disgusting thing I've ever seen... or smelled."

"What? What did I do?" he asked, clueless.

"Do you want something to eat or what?"

Geoff pondered, "Hmmm, how about a slice of pizza... with hot dogs, onions, and garlic. Extra garlic. It helps me fart."

And right on cue, he ripped a loud fart in Megan's direction.

"You're a pig, Geoff!"

"What? What did I do?" he smiled.

"Get out. Now!"

"Are you joking or..."

"I'm serious!" she said pointing to the door.

Just then, Freddy walked by and caught a whiff of Geoff's

fart. He covered his mouth and dry-heaved his way towards the bathroom. Geoff left and I was glad that I didn't have to deal with his antics (yet).

When I turned back around, Phil and Todd were back at it; chowder sampling Part II.

"Okay Phil, try it now. I think I added the missing ingredient."

Again, Phil took his time savoring every flavor. I still couldn't believe 'eat anything for a buck' Phil was Todd's go-to taste tester.

Finally, Phil gave Todd an approving thumbs up and announced, "By George, I think you got it!"

Just then, Freddy barged through the door, nearly knocking me over. He rushed over to Phil and Todd, excitedly babbling, "Did somebody say Boy George? I love Boy George!"

Freddy then busted into his version of "Karma Chameleon." By the time he got to "red, gold, and green," all of our eyes were staring blankly at him.

"What? Doesn't anyone here appreciate my many talents? Geez Louise!" he huffed. "And in case you guys were wondering, Steve, AKA hottie at table three, asked me if I wanted to meet him out for breakfast tomorrow morning." Freddy giggled and continued, "I told him to wake me up before you go-go!"

"Oh God!" said Todd. "That's gay, Freddy. Even for you."

Ignoring Todd's comment, Freddy continued to giggle and said, "And to be extra cute, I wrote down my number as 867-5309. You know, like the song?"

"You did give him your real number too, right?" I asked.

Freddy's giggling stopped, and he rushed back into the dining room.

***

By the time the afternoon rolled around, I gave up on trying to convince Todd that my intentions with Elise were completely legit. Why do I care what some negative, random cook thinks about me? I have nothing to prove to him regarding Elise, or regarding being the manager, or regarding anything!

Of course, being the type of person who hates when people don't like me or don't understand me, this was easier said than done. Okay, so I did care what Todd thought; what everyone thought, but in particular, what Elise thought. I was still thinking about what she said to me at her car; how she didn't want anything serious, and how she thought us going out would be a conflict of interest at work. The speech I was going to give her the next time I saw her was practically writing itself.

***

Around 4pm, my speech writing was forced to take a break. Another classic incident was about to take place at good ole Murphy's Oceanside. The lunch rush that day was busy and lasted longer than normal. By the time 4pm came, everyone was hurrying around getting everything ready for the dinner rush.

While I was helping Freddy rearrange some tables, Carl Jacobson entered and approached me. Carl was the longtime owner of the magazine shop down the road. As kids, we would go there in the summer to get our comics. As teenagers, his shop was our go-to for purchasing the new Rolling Stone or Spin magazines (& comics). We also loved those music magazines which had all the lyrics for the current, popular songs. Nothing was worse than knowing 97% of the lyrics to a song, but not being able to decipher that one line. Those magazines were our lifeline in the pre-internet/Google days.

"Hi, Mr. Jacobson. How's it going?" I asked.

"Not bad, Josh. Hey, have you guys seen Geoff around?"

"Oh God. What did he do now?" commented Megan as she walked by.

"I think he stole some magazines." Mr. Jacobson lowered his voice, "Some adult magazines."

Did I mention Mr. Jacobson's store sold adult magazines? Okay, confession: Comics and music magazines weren't the only reason we went in there. My first ever glimpse at a Juggs magazine was in his store. Even though we waited until his back was turned, or when he was busy with other customers, he always knew what we were up to. The giggling gave us away every time.

My nostalgic trip down *Porn-Mag Lane* was short-lived as a customer called out, "Hey, some weird guy locked himself in the bathroom and keeps laughing every time I knock."

It was déjà vu all over again (I suppose I didn't need to use the words *all over again*, the word déjà vu implies that). Anyway, just like before, I relied on our resident lock-picker to open the door. Phil used his paper clip, slid it back into his fanny pack (utility belt), saluted me, then walked off.

I took a deep breath and crossed my fingers that this wouldn't be another shit-incident. The good news was there was no face-melting stench like the other day. There was actually no smell at all except the pine cleaner we used in there.

I knocked twice and announced, "I'm coming in, Geoff. Okay?"

"Da ha ha ha," he laughed, "I'm touching my twang. Twaaaaang. Da ha ha ha."

Despite Geoff's warning, nothing could prepare me for what I was about to see. The good news: He wasn't naked this time... not completely. He still had his tank top on, but he stood in the corner with his shorts down around his ankles. The first thing my eyes were drawn to was his ass. His hairy, hairy, hairy ass. I hate to admit this, but in my head, I thought of my own weedwacker joke. Phil would have been proud.

The second thing my eyes were drawn to were the pages of the porn magazine strewn about everywhere. Everywhere. The final, and most disturbing, thing my eyes noticed was Geoff was still 'going at it.'

"Geoff! Stop that! Now!" I yelled. "I'm gonna shut the door and when I open it, your shorts better be pulled back up. Got it?"

I slammed the door shut.

"With your twang back in them," joked Megan over my shoulder. I shot her a look. She smiled and shrugged.

We waited while he finished up. And yes, I mean *finished up*. Surprisingly, Geoff exited the bathroom on his own volition, and even more surprising, he was fully dressed.

"You know I love ya, Geoff," I said, "but you are officially banned from ever using our bathrooms again! And no, I'm NOT joking, I'm serious." I then turned to Mr. Jacobson and said, "He's all yours."

He took Geoff by the arm and escorted him outside. When I turned back around, Megan and Freddy were standing there, each with money in their hands. I took their money, added a twenty to it, then said, "Go tell Phil cleanup on aisle six," I smiled.

Moments later, Phil approached the bathroom with cleaning supplies in his hand and forty bucks in his pocket. A look of awe came over his face as he opened the door and saw pages and pages of Playboy strewn all about.

"Whoa, what do we have here?" he smiled. "It's Miss July taped to the wall." Phil reached over and removed the page from the wall. "Oops," he laughed, "that's not tape." As I cringed in disgust, Phil looked at his cleaning products. "Looks like I'm gonna need a gizz mopper." I curiously looked at Phil. "A squeegee," he clarified.

Again, I cringed at the imagery. And speaking of imagery (& cringing), I watched Phil's eyes move from the scattered pages on the floor up to the ceiling.

"Jesus," he exclaimed, "Again with the ceiling? Not only does he have an ass cannon, but he has a super soaker for a dick." Phil stared at the ceiling and joked, "It's kind of like a mini stalactite." With that, he grabbed the squeegee.

"Oh, and Phil," I said before leaving, "throw the squeegee away after, okay? We don't need to be cleaning windows with that." Phil smiled, saluted me, then continued his cleaning.

14

"BLACK" – Pearl Jam

I have to admit, it was a little disappointing to not have Elise around to walk with after work. It did, however, allow me to perfect my speech to her. You know, the speech that would convince her to hang out with me more. I definitely needed a better angle than the whole non-date, date thing.

I had the following night off myself, so at least I avoided the end of the shift disappointment of her not being there. Doug also had the night off, so Pete and Scott came over to do a little pre-game drinking before we all headed out to Cap't Nick's for *Nickel Night.* That's right, nickel drafts! Being able to get shit-faced on the change you find in the couch cushions was a glorious thing.

Of course, like all good things in life, there was a catch. The "nickel draft keg" was usually tapped out before you could even drink a quarter's worth. In other words, you spent forty-five minutes getting buzzed on a quarter, and the rest of the night paying top dollar to get drunk. And then there's the buying drinks for friends... and girls... girls you know or otherwise.

It was ironic, we'd spend the whole week getting excited for *nickel night*, yet none of us would drop less than fifty bucks... some of us a hundred. Tonight's pre-game beer of choice was Rolling Rock. You can't start with something like Sam Adams or Heineken knowing that soon you'd be pounding down *nickel night* Natty Lights.

It was also commonplace for us to have a good *guy movie* on when we first started drinking for the night. Tonight's choice: 80s flick "Vision Quest." A coming of age story about a high school wrestler (Matthew Modine). Trust me, good stuff! Not only was it a great movie, but it had a stellar soundtrack too. Speaking of soundtracks, the closer it got to actually heading out to the bar, the movie would get muted and I'd pop in a kick-ass pre-bar mixtape. Don't judge... any of this.

Somewhere between "Vision Quest" and the mixtape being cranked up, I got an unexpected phone call from Megan at work. My first thought was, Oh God, please tell me Freddy didn't slap some guy's ass (again), or please don't tell me Geoff returned to the scene of his masturabutory crime.

Or please don't tell me Phil got rushed to the hospital for eating something he absolutely shouldn't have.

With all those crazy thoughts rushing through my head, I was more than pleasantly surprised to hear that Megan wanted to talk about Elise. Apparently, her Montreal trip was cut short. And not only was she already back in town, but she called the restaurant to see if we needed her to work tomorrow.

Yes, yes, and YES, I thought. I was a bit more reserved with my actual comments. I casually told Megan I wasn't sure, but to give me Elise's number and I'd call her and discuss it. I could sense that Megan was shaking her head at me, maybe even laughing at me, but I didn't really care. I was on my fourth Rolling Rock, so my confidence was pretty high. An 8.7 to be exact. Unfortunately, my babbling was at a 9.7.

Considering that Scott had Pearl Jam cranked up, I took the cordless phone into my bedroom and dialed. The first forty-seven seconds of our conversation actually went quite well. Elise told me the friend they drove with had a family emergency, so they were all forced to come back a day early. I then told her I thought tomorrow night was going to be extra busy (white lie), so if she wanted to work that would be great.

At the forty-seven second mark, she said she would definitely be there tomorrow night to work. For all intents and purposes, that should have been the end of the conversation, but... I did mention I was on my forth beer, right?

"So, listen Elise, I've been thinking about what you said the other night; about how it might be weird for us to hang out. And, well, I have to disagree. I know I'm a few years older than you, but maturity-wise I'm probably younger than you. And as far as me being your boss, it's not like I'd give you special treatment. Well, I did give you extra time off this week, but I would have done that for anyone. Bottom line, I just want to get to know you better, Elise. Nothing serious. And despite what you or anyone else might think, I'm <u>not</u> looking for just a hookup. And that's not just a line either. Well, I suppose it is a line... and I might have used that once or twice before, but I swear it's not a line in this case. Hooking up with you is the last thing on my mind. The last thing! Oh, not because you're ugly. God no! That's not what I meant."

I was sinking fast and I knew I had to end with a bang.

"I just want to hang out with you, Elise. Even if it's in a group setting like that first night. Yeah, that's it! We should totally do group dates! Not 'dates' per se, rather group get-togethers. Well, anyway, just think it over. I'll see you tomorrow. Bye."

I shit you not, I hung up the phone and actually thought, *That went pretty well.* Only in my twisted head could that conversation be considered *pretty well.* I should have been suspicious about the quietness coming from the other room, but I was too busy patting myself on my back for a job well done. It wasn't until I walked out of my room and saw their smirks that I knew I was in for it.

Scott starting in first, "Maturity-wise I'm probably younger than you?"

"I'm not looking to hook up with you? That's not a line, well maybe it is," Pete chimed in.

I then looked over to Doug.

"Go ahead, Doug," I urged. "Everyone else is making fun."

"I just have two words," smiled Doug. "Group dates?"

Everyone cracked up laughing. So much so, that they didn't hear me mumble, "Group get-togethers."

Needless to say, the rest of the night was filled with jokes at my expense. Luckily, I'd be too drunk to care.

15

"STRANGE ATTRACTION" – The Cure

Compared to the last week or so, the next couple of days were uneventful at the restaurant. There were no Freddy antics, no Geoff sightings, and even Phil was, dare I say, normal. Although, he did construct a giant spider web to catch flies (not to eat). The web was made completely out of, you guessed it, duct tape.

Even though the days were always unpredictable, the nights ended the same; with me walking Elise to her car. Not only did we talk and laugh about the events of the day, but I was usually able to work in some more questions on my list.

"Number seven: What was the first concert you ever went

to and what was your last?" I asked.

"Oh boy," she sighed. "You're totally going to make fun of me, aren't you?"

"Probably," I said.

"I was seventeen when I went to my first. My older sister Lesley took me and my friends to see..." she cringed. "I can't say it."

"It was New Kids on the Block, wasn't it?"

Her look said it all.

"Ha! I knew it," I laughed. "So, which one did you have a crush on?"

"Joey," she said bright-faced. "What about you?"

"Me? Oh I was definitely a Donnie guy."

"Ha. Ha. I meant what was your first concert?"

"U2. Their Joshua Tree tour," I said.

"Wow, you don't mess around, huh?" she said.

"Nope. So, what was your last concert?" I asked.

She hesitated a second then reluctantly said, "Boys II Men. Go ahead, crack your jokes."

"Nah, no judging here," I said. "Besides, I have the ultimate embarrassing concert."

"I'm listening," she smiled.

"Back in '91 a bunch of us went to the Club MTV Tour at Great Woods. Bell Biv Devoe, Tony! Toni! Tone! C&C Music Factory... Do I need to go on?" I said.

"Oh please do," she said. "I'm feeling better about my concerts by the minute."

"There might have been a Rico Suave sighting on stage," I said, head hung in shame. "It gets worse," I said.

"Is that possible?" she joked.

"Color Me Badd," I sighed.

"What did they sing again?" she asked.

"I Wanna Sex U Up", I mumbled.

"That's right! They're the *Tic toc ya, don't stop* guys," she excitedly said.

"Yeah. That's them," I said. "This stays between us, got it?"

"Ha. Don't worry, I'll keep it on the DDL," she winked.

While the mood was light, I decided to just go for it and test my group date idea. (Group get-togethers, I mean.)

"Hey, so tomorrow night a bunch of us are going out after work. Do you wanna come?" I said with fingers crossed. "We're going to that little Chinese restaurant next to the Aqua Lounge."

"The Golden Fortune Cookie? Nikki and I love that place."

"Tell her she's more than welcome to join us too."

"She probably has another date but I'll ask."

"So that's a yes? You'll go?" I asked with both fingers crossed.

"Sure, sounds fun." she said.

Exterior-Josh nodded cool and collective. While interior-Josh was high-fiving like a mother fucker. Now I just had to run this by everyone at work.

***

For obvious reasons, I didn't bother asking Todd if he wanted to join us. I asked Freddy, but he already had plans with his new flame, Steve. Ever since Freddy waited on him last week, they've been seeing each other non-stop. That just left Megan and Phil. Without them saying yes, this whole group get-together thing would be a lost cause.

I think Megan knew what I was up to and took pity on me. She had a sarcastic exterior, but deep down, Megan was a true sweetheart.

"I'll go, but you're fuckin' paying!" she said.

A true sweetheart, but a shrewd business woman.

***

Being a small family beach, most of the restaurants stopped serving food by 10pm. The Golden Fortune Cookie and Sun of a Beach were the exceptions. Considering that Sun of a Beach was just a takeout window, we chose The Golden Fortune Cookie. They served drinks and food right up until 1am. The place was fairly tiny; ten tables max. The business was owned and run by Mr. & Mrs. Wong.

The best way to describe Mr. Wong is that he was a 5'0" Chinese version of Freddy. He was dressed flashy in a green dress jacket adorned with sequins. The only thing more sparkly was his giant white-toothed smile. Even his animated exuberance rivaled that of Freddy. The big difference being: Mr. Wong had a wife and Freddy had a Steve.

"Hello, my friends," he smiled, handing us menus, "and welcome to The Golden Fortune Cookie. Do you like my new jacket? Mrs. Wong bought it for my birthday last week."

He turned to the kitchen window and gave his wife a proud thumbs up.

"It looks like they threw a leprechaun and some glitter into a blender," Phil mumbled.

Megan and Elise shot him a glare. I was more shocked he didn't work in a squirrel/weedwacker reference.

Mr. Wong was unsure how to react, but he continued to smile and asked, "Can I start you off with some drinks? The Wong's specialty maybe? *Shaolin Punch*! It goes down smooth like a fruit punch, but hits you harder than a Bruce Lee kick to the head. Keee Yaah!"

With that, he snapped off a leg kick high in the air. It wasn't just for show either. It could have done some serious damage. We all looked at each other in shock.

"Um, I think I'll just have a Sam Adams," I hesitantly said. Megan and Elise nodded for the same as me.

Phil pondered, looked at the drink menu and said, "The Grape Grasshopper… does that have real grasshoppers in it?"

Mr. Wong slowly shook his head no.

"Oh," Phil sighed disappointedly. "Umm, does that

Shaolin Punch have alcohol in it?"

Mr. Wong excitedly nodded, but before he could list all the liquors in it, Phil sighed. "I'll have the non-alcoholic version of that," Phil said matter-of-factly.

Mr. Wong's smile faded. "But that would just be fruit punch," he said.

"Perfect!" Phil exclaimed. "Oh, and can I get one of those fancy umbrellas?"

Did I mention that Phil doesn't drink alcohol, or smoke, or do drugs? One can only imagine the things he'd eat or say if he did.

Mr. Wong looked disappointed that none of us wanted his Shaolin Punch (with alcohol).

"You not like a Bruce Lee?" he questioned.

I immediately thought of Elise's love for Kung Fu movies.

"Funny you should ask that," I said looking at Elise. That's as far as I got before she playfully elbowed me.

"Very well, three beers and a fruit punch... with an umbrella," he said smiling and shaking his head.

After he walked off, Phil said, "Is it me or does he remind you of..."

"A short Chinese Freddy?" Megan finished.

We watched Mr. Wong give his wife a kiss and then we all said in unison, "But straight."

"Speaking of Freddy," said Elise, "I thought he was coming tonight?"

"Pfft, he's on another date with that Steve dude," scoffed

Phil.

"Aww, no hot date for you tonight, Phil?" Elise smiled.

"Nah. Between building my new potato gun and trying to figure out the square root of yellow, I just don't have the time."

Two weeks ago, Phil's 'square root of yellow' comment would have left me dumbfounded, but now I just chalked it up as Phil being Phil.

"Do you really shoot potatoes out of that?" Elise asked.

"Nah. Golf balls, rocks, blueberry muffins, squirrels."

"Do you ever act fuckin' normal?" questioned Megan.

"Only on days that don't end in Y," Phil retorted.

As weird as Phil was, and he was pretty damn weird, he definitely added ample entertainment on our group date… um, group get-together.

At the end of the night, Megan made sure to slide the bill my way. Being able to spend an extra two hours after work with Elise was worth every penny. Megan also slid the little Buddha salt and pepper shakers Elise's way. Elise had been admiring them all night.

"Go ahead, slip them in your purse," whispered Megan.

Unsure, Elise hesitated, but when the coast was clear, she discreetly and nervously put them in her purse.

Megan saw how nervous she was and laughed, "You've never stolen anything in your life, have you?"

Elise blushed and said, "Not even a candy bar."

Just then, Mr. Wong approached to collect the money.

Elise did her best to not make eye contact. Her fingers did this nervous tapping thing on the table. Dare I say, her fidgeting was kind of adorable. There were many moments that summer when I'd look at Elise and feel completely smitten. And happy. Happily smitten, if you will. This was one of those moments.

When she finally did make eye contact with him, he read her guilt like a book. He slowly looked from her eyes over to where the salt and pepper shakers used to be. I tried to diffuse the moment by handing Mr. Wong a big tip as we all stood up to leave.

He gave me a slight bow, and before he headed back to the kitchen, he quietly said these words.

"Remember what Confucius say: "Every breath you take, every move you make, I'll be watching you. I'll be watching you."

He gave each of us a polite smile then turned to leave. Needless to say, as soon as Mr. Wong was out of sight, Elise returned the shakers to the table. By the time we were all out on the sidewalk, her face was still red with embarrassment.

"Good thing Freddy isn't here. He'd be shocked to learn that Sting stole his lyrics from Confucius." I joked.

"Well, come on," Megan said motioning to Phil, "I'll give you a ride. We'll see you guys tomorrow. Thanks again for paying, bossman." She gave me a wink as Phil gave me his typical salute and then they were off.

As luck would have it, Elise was parked in the opposite

direction as Megan. Opposite as Megan, but the same as me. Hmmm, it's as if I planned it. As I began walking her to her car, she also thanked me for paying and then started to tell me, "You really don't have…"

"To walk you to your car?" I finished. "I know, Elise, but I want to. Besides…" I smiled pulling out my trusty list.

She laughed out loud (ten years from now that would be known as LOL). "You're ridiculous," she continued to laugh. "Do you carry that everywhere?"

"No! Maybe," I smiled. "Shall I pick or do you want to?"

She rolled her brown eyes and said, "How about number thirty-one?"

I flipped the paper over and glanced down the page until I came to thirty-one.

"I might add a little bit to this one," I said. "Originally, it was going to be name one of your favorite childhood memories. But how about in honor of your grandfather, you name your favorite memory with him?"

I wasn't sure how she'd react to my alteration, but as soon as I saw her warmly smile and ponder, I knew she was more than okay with it.

"It's a Wonderful Life," she said.

"What?" I curiously asked.

"The movie. Have you ever seen it?"

"Only sixty-two times or so," I laughed. "It's one of my favorite Christmas-time movies. Well, that and Rudolph."

"Aww, I loved Rudolph," she said. "And the Island of

Misfit Toys rocked! Actually," she giggled, "when I was little and got mad at my parents, I used to threaten I was gonna run away to the island and live with the rest of the misfits."

"And just think," I smiled, "now you get to work on the Island of Misfits."

Elise laughed, "Yeah, we do have quite the strange crew, huh? All we need now is for a Charlie in the Box to show up for a job."

"Or a train with square wheels," I added.

"And what was the deal with that cute little dolly?" she asked. "They never explained why she was a misfit, did they?"

I stopped walking and carefully thought about her question. I did a quick mental checklist of all the misfit toys and what made them misfits, but I couldn't for the life of me remember what was wrong with the little dolly. If this was ten years from now, I could have just googled that shit, but only being 1995, we were left to simply rack our brains.

"I think you're right, Elise, they never did explain it. I guess it's kinda like Bigfoot or the Loch Ness Monster or the Bermuda Triangle... a mystery... an enigma... a conundrum... an abstruseness, if you will."

The thesaurus in me could have gone on, but I noticed her giving me that look - that Elise look. The one that said, 'What is wrong with you, Josh?' I deflected her look by changing the subject back to my original question.

"So how does 'It's a Wonderful Life' tie into your favorite childhood memory with your grandfather again?" I asked.

"It was Grampa's all-time favorite Christmas movie. My nana never made it past twenty minutes before falling asleep. A few weeks before Christmas, my sisters and I would spend the night at their house and help them decorate."

"Their house here in York," I asked.

"No. Their place here is just a summer cottage. Their real house is in the same town in Vermont where I'm from, Stowe. Anyway, the whole decorating the tree and baking cookies thing was kind of my sisters' and Nana's thing. My sisters and I would spend the whole afternoon listening to Christmas music while stringing popcorn and cranberries for the tree. In the evening, my sisters went into the kitchen to help Nana bake and decorate cookies. Baking was never my thing, so I'd always go in the den and cuddle with Grampa and watch 'It's a Wonderful Life.' I have to admit, for the longest time, I never really liked, understood, or paid attention to it. And if truth be told, for years I'd usually fall asleep halfway through it. I just liked drinking eggnog and cuddling with him. I absolutely hate smoking of any kind, but... even to this day I can't help but smile when I catch a whiff of someone's cigar smoke. Silly, I know."

The ocean breeze picked up, and Elise brushed her hair from her eyes. As the street light caught her face, her sad, nostalgic, innocent look created another 'moment.' One I wouldn't soon forget. Seconds later, she continued her story.

"Considering there was a big age gap between me and my older sisters, eventually it was just me going over Nana and Grampa's house to help decorate. By then, the movie had totally grown on me. Do you know the part at the end when Harry toasts to his big brother 'the richest man in town'?"

I nodded yes.

"No matter how many times he'd seen the movie, that part would always make Grampa tear up." She paused and sadly looked away. "This was the first year we didn't get to watch it together."

"I'm sorry," was all I could say to her.

"It's okay," she said.

Nothing was said as we made our way towards her car. It wasn't until she started to unlock her door that she finally spoke.

"Thanks again for the walk. And for the food and drinks earlier too."

"Yeah, of course," I replied. "Well, goodnight, Elise."

"Night, Josh," she said as she climbed in her car.

She gave me a wave and shut the door. She began to back the car up but stopped. She rolled down her window and sweetly said, "Thanks for the question. It was a good one."

Before I could ruin the moment with my whole babbling thing, she rolled the window up and drove off. This time when her taillights faded, I smiled, knowing I did good. Elise still wasn't ready to let me read her whole life story, but for now, for tonight, I was just glad she let me read a chapter.

16

"STRANGELOVE" – Depeche Mode

The next couple of nights, Nikki picked Elise up after work, so I didn't get a chance to walk her to her car. I did use a few lulls throughout the day to ask her some more questions on my list. Considering we were at work, I kept them simple.

My last question of the day was the simplest, yet, her answer threw me for a loop - in a good way.

"Okay, Elise, what is your all-time favorite food?" I asked.

Without hesitation she answered, "Cap'n Crunch. With the crunchberries," she added.

"You're joking, right?" I laughed.

"No. I love that stuff. I mean, it definitely shreds the crap out of the roof of your mouth, but it's totally worth it."

It was finally time for me to give Elise the crazy look she had given me (many times). I looked at her, shook my head and walked off.

"With crunchberries," I chuckled as I headed over to Freddy.

Freddy had his own look going on at me. His look was... sweet? Adoring? Creepy? Yes, all of the above.

"Ohhh Joshua, I think it's so romantical how you wrote a whole list of questions to get to know Elise better."

As Freddy swooned, Todd scoffed from the grill area.

"And by 'getting to know' you actually mean 'trying to bang'."

Freddy was quick to defend me. "I don't like your attitude, Mr. Grumpypants. Just because you don't have a romantical bone in your body, doesn't mean I'm going to let you suck the romance out of me!"

"Trust me, Freddy," Todd said, "I'm not sucking ANYTHING out of you!"

"Oh youuuuuuuuuu," giggled Freddy.

***

I earlier compared Murphy's to the Island of Misfit Toys, and what happened next only cemented that belief. Megan and I stood off to the side and watched as three young kids ran rough-shot around the dining room. The whole time their parents sat idly by saying nothing. It wasn't that they were oblivious to their kids' actions, they were well aware of their little maniacs. They just happened to think it was funny, cute even. What the fuck is cute about three kids (all under six) running around playing tag in a public restaurant? We watched them weaving in and out, and at one point, they seemed to be playing duck, duck, goose around an older couple, who were just trying to enjoy their fish 'n' chips.

"I'm never having kids!" Megan said as their voices raised to a high-pitched shrill. Their shrill reminded me of the time a spider crawled on Freddy's foot.

Phil exited the bathroom just as their voices hit a ten on the obnoxious scale. The table directly in front of us sat three girls all in their early twenties. Two of them were dressed fairly normal. The other one was dressed mostly in black including her lipstick. Her hair had blue streaks dyed in it, and she had multiple piercings; at least ten that I could visibly see. One could only assume there were other hidden ones.

Her comment regarding the kids couldn't have been timed any better. Just as Phil walked by she said, "Jesus, someone should duct tape those little shits to their chairs. They're like a bunch of squirrels on acid."

Her friends stared blankly at her. The SAME blank look we give to Phil! The words duct tape and squirrel stopped Phil dead in his size fourteen shoes. He looked over at the girl and then at the kids.

"Looks like that one kid used a weedwacker to cut his hair," Phil said.

The girl with the blue hair cracked up laughing. Her friends joined me and Megan in giving both of them blank looks. Phil joined her in laughing and then it happened: Their eyes met.

She smiled her black-lipstick smile and said, "I'm Marissa."

"I'm Phil," he replied (and saluted her).

After witnessing this strange, warped love connection, Freddy rushed over to Megan and me and gushed, "Awww, I smell a romance brewing."

And right on cue, a long, loud fart boomed from behind us.

"Da ha ha ha, and now you smell my fart!" Geoff laughed.

The fart (and stench) was a direct hit on Freddy.

He cringed, covering his nose and mouth as he muffled, "Oh my God, Geoff! It smells like beef jerky and Cheez-Its."

Needless to say, Freddy rushed off, dry heaving all the way into the bathroom. This caused a chain reaction. Hearing the fart noise caused the demon-kids to hit an eleven on the obnoxious scale, and in turn, it caused Geoff to *da ha ha ha* even louder. Like I said, Island of fucking Misfit Toys!

17

"LIPS LIKE SUGAR" – Echo & the Bunnymen"

The next time I walked Elise to her car was one of my favorite walks and talks all summer. The normal five minute walk to her car turned into over an hour of us talking. An hour and seven minutes to be exact.

"So what did you say you majored in again?" I asked.

"Social work," she answered.

"Ah, so your goal is to work at an underpaid and underappreciated job?" I joked.

"You're not wrong," she chuckled. "Sometimes I wonder if I'm making the right decision, but... I just like helping people, especially ones that can't help themselves." She saw my smile widen. "That sounds dorky, doesn't it?"

"Not at all," I said. "This world needs more people like that. I actually admire the hell outta you."

"Ha. Let's not go overboard there, killer," she smiled. "But it's definitely a tough field. Last summer I did this internship at a home for troubled and mentally challenged kids. It was the hardest, most stressful thing I've ever done."

"Troubled and mentally challenged kids, huh? Sounds like my job now."

"Da ha ha ha," she laughed imitating Geoff. "Trust me, as weird as our crew is, it's a cake walk compared to the real deal."

"I'm sure it is," I nodded. "Like I said, the world needs more people like you." She offered an appreciative smile as I continued. "So if you come here every summer to visit your grandparents how come I haven't seen you around?" I asked.

"I actually haven't been here since high school. Throughout college, I worked my ass off back in Stowe to help pay for school. I worked as a chambermaid at one of the mountain resorts. After I graduated in May, my parents urged me to come to York Beach for the summer; a celebration of me graduating, I guess. I'm sure they also wanted my nana to have company, especially seeing as this is her first summer here without Grampa."

We reached her car and I knew it was only a matter of time before she pulled her keys out, signaling me it was time for her to go. But for now, her keys stayed in her purse. And to my surprise, she actually turned the tables and started asking me questions.

"So what about you?" she asked. "Is the restaurant field your thing?"

"I don't know about 'my thing', but it's pretty much what I know."

"Do you want to own your own one day?" she asked.

"Maybe," I shrugged. "I'm not sure about a restaurant though. Maybe something more laid back like a coffee shop. Either that or a strip club."

"Da ha ha ha, are you joking or serious?" she laughed as she pulled out her keys from her purse.

My smile quickly faded into disappointment. I didn't want her to leave yet. Just as quickly, however, my disappointment turned into a relieved smile. She only opened the door to retrieve a sweatshirt and a Red Sox hat. There's something about a cute girl in a Red Sox hat that makes her... cuter. Especially a real Sox hat and not a pink one. I was so smittenly entranced that I didn't even hear her question.

"Uh, hello?" she said.

"I'm sorry," I said snapping out of it. "What did you ask me?"

"I said why don't you just do it? Open up your own place."

I shrugged and said, "I just haven't found the right situation. Actually, that's not true. I really haven't even looked. I haven't had the time to look. Eh, that's not true either. I've had plenty of time. I guess it's just a combination of procrastination and fear of failure. Sometimes it seems like I spend my time just watching from the sidelines, ya know?"

"You?" she questioned. "You seem so motivated... so upbeat... so..."

"Talkative?" I added.

"I was going to say positive, but talkative works too," she laughed.

Her laugh was followed by a silence. Before it turned into a silence of the uncomfortable variety, I jumped in with a question.

"I have a question for you," I said.

"What number is this one?" she smiled.

"Actually, it's not on my list. I just thought of it."

"Whoa! Going unscripted, huh?"

"Yeah, something like that," I said. "Earlier you said your parents urged you to come here as a celebration for graduating." She nodded. "So why not just take it off job free? I'm sure you earned it. Especially having a friend here with you. Does Nikki have a summer job here too?"

Elise laughed out loud, "Nikki? She probably doesn't have to work the rest of her life. Her family has more money than God. They live down in the richest part of Connecticut."

"Ahh, Yankee country," I said looking at her hat.

Elise nodded and snarled, "Don't even get me started."

"So how do you girls know each other?" I asked.

"I met Nikki my junior year in college. We were one of the few New Englanders, so I guess that helped us bond."

"Ahh," I said. "So, back to my summer job versus no summer job question."

"Well, my original plan was to do as you suggested; take the summer off and just relax and enjoy myself, but..."

I interrupted, "But you heard I was running Murphy's, huh?"

"Yeah, something like that," she said rolling her eyes. "Actually, my dad got laid off from his job a week after I got here. He's been with the company for over twenty years."

"I'm sorry, that must suck." I said.

"He'd never show it, but my mom says he's pretty stressed out and depressed over it. When my mom told me, my first impulse was to head back to Stowe, ya know, for moral support. But she told me if I left the beach to come home, it would make him feel even worse. So I know it's only five or six weeks, and I'm probably not gonna make enough money to make a difference, but I'd just feel so guilty if I just sat on the beach every day. Especially knowing he was sitting home jobless and depressed."

I looked at her and slowly shook my head.

"What?" she asked.

"That might be the sweetest thing I've ever heard. Most people in that situation would have just plopped their asses down on the beach every day."

"Really? Would you?" she asked.

"Me? No. I would have done exactly what you're doing. But I'm not like most people."

This caused her to laugh.

"Sorry," she said containing herself, "I'm not saying you're not, but you do realize that every person thinks they're not like most people."

I thought about that for a second then nodded in agreement. She was right. She was absolutely right. Everyone thinks they're not like the 'others', which ultimately makes them exactly like the others.

"That being said," I smirked, "I'm still not like most people."

"Good for you," she joked then glanced at her watch. "Well, I should get going."

I desperately wanted her to stay and keep talking, but I knew asking her to stay longer would come across as needy and pathetic, and I never want to come across as that. After all, I'm not like most people, right? Begging her to stay was out of the question - definitely out of the question. So I didn't. I stalled her instead.

"It was pretty fun the other night at The Golden Fortune Cookie, huh?"

"Yeah, it was," she smiled.

"Because it was a group thing, right?" I asked.

I probably shouldn't have mentioned that, but like I said, I was stalling. Also, as you know, I'm not always so careful with my comments,. I could tell she felt uneasy as she searched for the right response. I should have bailed her out, but my next comment only made her feel more guilty.

"No, no, it's fine. I'm not cool enough to go out with one-on-one, but whatever, it's fine."

It was obvious to me that I was just making light of the situation. It's what I do. It was also obvious that she really did feel uneasy and unsure how to respond.

"I'm just kidding, Elise." I finally said. "I'll take what I can get from you. Whoa! That sounded kinda pervy, but I totally meant it in the most innocent way possible. I just want to hang out with you. Even if it's to walk you to your car at night. And yes, even if it's a group date, umm, group get-together. As a matter of fact, I'm gonna dedicate the rest of the summer to being the best group activities planner around!"

Elise's uneasy look was replaced with the all too familiar, 'you're such a dork' look. Her comment to me as she smiled and shook her head was also familiar.

"You're ridiculous!" she laughed and then got in her car.

"You do realize, every time you say that to me, I take it as a compliment, right?" I smiled.

"Of course you do," she smirked as she started her car. "You're different than most, right? Night, Josh. See you tomorrow."

"Goodnight, Elise."

18

"BLISTER IN THE SUN" – Violent Femmes

So, as promised, over the next couple of weeks I turned into the master planner of group get-togethers. In most cases, they were more like group activities. At times, I felt like a camp counselor planning out fun activities for the week. Sometimes only one person joined Elise and I. Sometimes a few did. Todd never did. Still though, Todd and I had actually developed a not-so-horrible working relationship.

I know what you're thinking, if all these workers are all hanging out together during the day then who's running the restaurant? Our staff actually consisted of a dozen or so workers. I only chose to write about a handful of them because, well, honestly, the rest of them weren't that exciting. They weren't bad people or even bad workers, they were just sort of there. They did their jobs and went home.

Anyway, back to my group activities. What were some of them, you ask? Great question. One afternoon, Elise, Nikki, Megan, Freddy, and a couple of my friends all went bridge jumping down at the Cape Neddick bridge. What made it truly memorable was watching Freddy turn the activity into a spectacle.

Let's start with his bridge jumping attire. It consisted of scuba goggles, purple Zinka on his nose, and bright lime green flippers. And considering he never actually jumped in, all of which was an overkill.

"Ok, ok, ok, I'm gonna do it, I'm gonna do it," he repeated as he inched closer to the edge. Only to follow that with, "I can't, I can't, I can't."

He did this not once, not twice, but five times. Even though Freddy never jumped in, as usual, he made the afternoon that much more memorable. Whether it was video games and foosball at the Fun-O-Rama, or watching Freddy do karaoke at night, the simpler the activity, the more fun we had.

Speaking of karaoke, Freddy and his friends are crazy good, especially on their home turf. Yup, you guessed it, Megan, Elise and I attended karaoke night at the famous Oqunquit bar known as the Fuzzy Banana. And it was a fucking blast! Elise made it crystal clear to me and Freddy that she would only go if we promised not to force her on stage again.

Personally, I wanted to give her the speech. The one that said, *you shouldn't be embarrassed about your talent, and if I had your voice, I'd be on stage every chance I'd got.* But I didn't. I knew she was uncomfortable with the spotlight, and I didn't want to do anything to prevent her from hanging out for the night.

Despite Elise's specific orders, Freddy had a secret plan to bring her up on stage anyway and do a duet with him. When I caught wind of his plan, I begged him not to go through with it. There was NO way I wanted to jeopardize future get-togethers with Elise. And because of that, I was forced to make a deal with the devil; the gay devil. The only way Freddy would agree not to drag Elise up was if I took her place. Needless to say, I was Sonny and Freddy was Cher as we did the weirdest version of "I Got You Babe."

The things we do for love.

As much as I wanted a real one-on-one date with Elise, I have to admit, our group get-togethers were fun, and I suppose it did take the pressure off a bit. If it was just the two of us, awkward silences would usually lead to me babbling like a fool about God knows what. With a group, especially our group, there was never an awkward silence; just awkward conversations. And compared to Freddy, Phil, or even Megan, my conversations seemed quite normal.

19

"GLYCERINE" - Bush

Between working so much at Murphy's and hanging out with everyone from work, I barely saw my friends. But by the lack of shit I got from them, it was obvious that they were also busy doing their own thing. One of the reasons I chose the summer of '95 for this book was because that summer sort of marked the beginning of the end of a lot of friendships. I'm not trying to be overly dramatic; friendships didn't 'end', but rather started to naturally fade.

If this was the summer of '93, our *summer crew* would have consisted of about twenty of us or so; guys and girls and 90% of us were single. Whether it was a bar, a club, a party, or just at the beach, we would probably hang out five nights a week together.

Inevitably, time changes everything, and serious relationships and real jobs all start to take precedence. Some of our local friends moved away, and some of our summer friends stopped coming up to York all together. I suppose growing up and growing apart is a natural occurrence, but I definitely noticed it more this summer than ever before.

Random hookups and fly-by-night summer romances were now replaced with serious relationships, commitments... kids even. Silly summer jobs were replaced by careers, and that summer crew of twenty crazy kids had slowly dwindled down to a handful, at best. And those five nights a week partying was lucky to be five times a summer.

A few of us, however, did get a chance to get together on Thursday for $.25 draft night at the Aqua Lounge. I know I said earlier that Thursday nights were nickel night over at Cap't Nick's, so you're probably thinking, why pay a quarter for a beer when you can pay a nickel? Good question, but the answer is pretty simple: Cap't Nick's is two towns over, so there's that whole issue about finding a designated driver. And considering we rarely went out together anymore, it would be a shame for one of us to not be able to partake in the alcoholic festivities.

The Aqua Lounge, on the other hand, was in the heart of York Beach and was walking (stumbling) distance from most of our houses, and at the very least, it was stumbling distance to the beach. There was many a night that we simply crashed on the sand. You just had to make sure you were up by sunrise because that's when the giant, loud beach grader would drive along the sand clearing the beach of seaweed (and of drunk idiots).

Despite the Aqua Lounge being one of the few bars/clubs in town, we usually only found ourselves there on quarter draft night. Once we all hit twenty-one, downtown Portsmouth was the place to be. Portsmouth was only about a fifteen minute drive from York, and its historic downtown is lined with dozens of cool bars and clubs, all walking distance from each other.

With multiple bars comes a variety of women. And when you're swinging single, variety is a must. If you're striking out at the Rusty Hammer, a trip across the street to the State Street Saloon might be just the scenery change you need to get your mojo back (not usually, but it's a good theory).

Like I said earlier, besides quarter night, the Aqua Lounge was known for its two under twenty-one nights. So, before we all hit the big twenty-one, the Aqua Lounge was THE place to be.

I'm not ashamed to admit (well maybe a little), despite my strong preference to the more sad, alternative-type music, I sort of went through a brief Hip Hop, dance music phase. Mostly this phase was relegated to the under twenty-one nights at the Aqua Lounge.

It was much easier showing off for the summer girls when

you had sweet dance moves. Nothing says sexy more than seeing a nineteen year old trying to do the MC Hammer shuffle while wearing the prerequisite parachute pants, right? Seriously, what's hotter than a kid wearing an acid-washed jean jacket with a skull cap on doing his best Rico Suave moves? And if someone had something negative to say about it, I'd just tell them to STEP OFF... 'cause I'm doing the Hump... the Humpty Hump! Word!

Anyway, on this particular quarter night, Pete, Scott, Doug, and myself decided to bail before last call. We walked across the street to shoot some late night hoops at the court. A few things you could always count on from our late night hoops' sessions:

1) All of us jumping up and seeing who could touch higher on the net. Even drunk, Scott always won.

2) Pete standing at half court, counting the pretend clock down for a last second half court heave (6% success-rate).

3) My strange infatuation with trying to bounce the ball off the pavement and into the basket. WTF?

4) Doug hitting ONE shot in a row and announcing how great he shoots when he's drunk.

5) Doug making us form a circle and doing the Harlem Globetrotter's passing drills.

The darkness of the courts combined with our alcohol levels made for a very interesting sight for cars driving by. More times than not, our 'no-look passes' turned into a 'no-catch' pass. Unless you consider getting hit in the head or the nuts as catching it. So, if you were driving by the courts late at night in the summer and saw three or four drunk white idiots doing the Harlem Globetrotter's passing drill, chances were good it was us. Ridiculous, stupid, and utterly silly, but… I fuckin' loved every moment of it.

"So Josh, how're your *group dates* going?" Doug asked.

I almost made it the whole night without anyone bringing that up. Almost.

"Group dates? What's that all about?" Scott asked me.

Doug had no problem answering for me. "Don't you remember, Scott? Our boy Josh has a major crush on some chick at work, but she'll only go out with him in a group setting."

"Oh yeaaah," Scott answered. "That Elise chick."

I didn't need to look up to know that everyone was staring at me like I had lost my mind. I did my best to explain the situation, but the more I explained it out loud, the more I realized that maybe I HAD lost my mind.

"I just don't get why you're working so hard at this one," Doug rambled. "Considering you just got out of a relationshit, I don't know why you'd wanna jump back in. I'd just be having some fun if I were you. And by fun, I mean…"

"We all know what you mean, Doug," I said as I tried to bounce the ball in from the foul line.

I missed by a mile and was forced to chase the ball into to empty parking lot which gave me time to think about Doug's question. He might be a pain in the ass sometimes, but his question was a legitimate one.

Why was I working so hard on getting to know Elise? The list of questions, the group-togethers, the walk to her car every night... why???

From the outside looking in, you might think it was just the attraction of wanting something you can't have, or maybe the challenge of being the one who knocks down her walls.

And before all you girls out there go judging and laughing at me, it's really no different than dating a *bad boy* in hopes of being the one who 'changes' him. How did that work out for you? Huh? I'll tell you how; 91% of the time you're not only left with an unchanged D-bag, but you ended up wasting months/years of your life doing so. So there!

The truth is, my pursuit of Elise went beyond just looking at her as a challenge, and it also went beyond just being attracted to her. There was just something about her that I couldn't put my finger on. And there lies the answer, I think. I returned to the court ready to respond to Doug's question.

"First of all, Doug, Liz and I didn't have a relationshit. It ended naturally. It just ran its course. And secondly, I'm not really sure why I'm trying so hard with Elise, but I think it's because she has the *it* factor."

The three of them looked at each other, and Doug said what they all were thinking.

"What the fuck is the *it* factor?"

I knew better than to engage in this type of conversation with three drunk dudes... on a basketball court... late o'clock at night. But I did it anyway.

"If I asked you guys to list the top five things you look for in a girl... and if I found ten girls who each had all five of those qualities, it doesn't mean you'd be compatible with any of them."

"I call bullshit," exclaimed Doug.

I should have quit right there, but I didn't. I turned and addressed Pete.

"Pete, do you have your list of five things in your head?" I asked. He pondered a moment then nodded. "Ok, so how many of those things does Michelle have?"

Pete shrugged and said, "Maybe two or three."

"Are those two or three things the reason you were attracted to her?" I asked.

Doug and Scott stopped shooting and looked intently at Pete. It was as if his answer would be a make or break for my *it factor* argument.

"I guess they're a part of it." Pete said. "I don't know, I can't really put my finger on why I fell for her."

"You can't put your finger on it because she just had *it...* as in the *it factor*. I rest my case," I proudly said.

All three of them looked at each other, shrugged, then conceded. They didn't actually come out and admit that I was right, but they certainly stopped arguing otherwise. We continued to shoot around for a bit, and it wasn't until we were leaving that Scott brought up the Elise thing again.

"So even if she has the *it factor*," began Scott, "didn't you say she was leaving in August? So unless you're just looking for a summer fling, then what's the point?"

Drunk people aren't supposed to ask hard hitting questions, are they? Again, I had to stop and think a second before responding.

"I don't really know what I want or expect from this," I said. "I do know I love hanging out with her. But I also know she's leaving for Vermont soon, and even if she wasn't, I don't know if it'd amount to anything anyway. She's a tough nut to crack. She lets me in only so far then shuts down."

Doug smirked, "She only lets you stick your dick in so far then she shuts down?"

All three of them cracked up laughing. I started to take the high road, but then I whipped the ball at his nuts.

From there, we decided to walk to Scott's house and crash. He lived at the end of Long Sands Beach. It was a fairly long hike, but it gave us the opportunity for one of our walkabouts.

As far back as I can remember, the four of us would take these walkabouts. It didn't matter what time in the night or what time of the year. Some of our best ones were during snow storms in the dead of winter.

It didn't always include all of us. Sometimes it was only three, sometimes just two of us. The walkabouts didn't always involve being drunk either. It was just a chance for us to walk and talk. You know, about important guy stuff.

"I still can't believe you're moving to Florida," Scott said.

"I can't believe you're fucking getting married," Doug said with an offended tone. "The same cereal for the rest of your life?"

Pete was quick to shoot him a look.

"I love Michelle and all," Doug continued, "but come on, dude! Do you really want to have cornflakes the rest of your life?"

"Who says Michelle is like cornflakes?" asked Pete.

"What is she like then?" smiled Scott.

Pete wasn't going to dignify him with an answer until he saw all three of us were intently awaiting a comparison.

Finally, Pete caved. "I guess Michelle would be like Cinnamon Toast Crunch."

Draw your own conclusions, but his answer pleased all of us greatly. It was at that point on our walkabout that we took turns comparing sex with certain girls to cereals. Although the actual phrase TMI wouldn't gain popularity for years to come, I am positive it originated with Doug and his comments.

"Remember that girl I dated last winter? The one that worked at the Draft House?" Doug asked.

"Wacky Jackie?" asked Scott.

Doug nodded.

"Wasn't she just a one night stand?" I said.

"A four night stand," Doug corrected.

"I'd hardly call that dating," I laughed.

"Semantics," he shrugged.

"No offense," said Pete, "but she was kind of nasty."

All of us including Doug shook our heads in agreement.

Scott smiled and asked, "What kind of cereal was she?"

Without thinking about his answer, Doug said, "Shredded Wheat."

Although we were tempted to ask him why, we knew if we did, he would tell us... in full detail. He did leave us with a disgustingly vivid parting shot.

"And when she was turned on, it was more like soggy shredded wheat. Yup, like soggy frosted mini wheats."

The next thirty seconds were spent walking in silence with Doug's imagery dancing in our heads and in the pit of our stomachs. It was Pete who spoke first and said what we were all thinking.

"If she was like shredded wheat..."

"Soggy shredded wheat," added Scott.

"If she was like *soggy shredded wheat*," corrected Pete, "then why was it a four night stand rather than just a one and done?"

Doug's answer was short and matter of fact. "Some cereals you need to acquire a taste for them. Sadly, Jackie was not one of them. Not at all!! Thankfully, the new girl I've been seeing is more like Lucky Charms," Doug proudly boasted.

I'll spare you guys the details on this one. Trust me, it's for the best.

"A new girl, huh?" I said. "I've been wondering why I

haven't seen you around the apartment lately."

"We've been dating a solid two weeks now," Doug explained.

"Is she old enough to get into R rated movies?" asked Scott.

"For your information, dickhead, she's thirty… and a nurse… a hot nurse. Guys, I'm thinking she might be the one. She's perfect."

All three of us looked incredulously at Doug.

"I'm serious," he said.

And for a brief moment we all looked at Doug in awe. Our best friend might actually be in love.

"I don't even have to give her the head tap, she just goes down on me on her own," he eagerly pointed out.

It's pathetic that Doug's main requirement for the perfect girl was something so juvenile. It was also pathetic that the rest of us were more than slightly intrigued and impressed with this information.

"No head tap? Really?" asked Pete.

"Nope!" smiled Doug. "I'm telling you, I have this gut feeling that this could be love. Yup, true love."

20

"HEY JEALOUSY" – Gin Blossoms

"Fuck true love! And fuck my gut feeling!" slurred a drunk Doug three nights later.

Doug had stumbled into the restaurant around closing time babbling about his breakup with the hot nurse. I already had plans that night with Elise, Freddy, and Elise's friend, Nikki, but as the guy code states: *No man left behind.* Especially a heartbroken, drunk one.

At the last minute, Freddy ended up bailing and going out with Steve. That just left a foursome. Doug relented at first, but when I told him we were going to the Golden Fortune Cookie, he was all in. Chinese food is a great remedy for a broken heart. That, and more alcohol.

It was my first time hanging out with Nikki,, and I have to say, it was kind of weird. It wasn't that I didn't like her, not at all. She was actually quite funny in a snarky kind of way. I guess I felt she was judging me, sizing me up, if you will.

I assumed Elise had told her about my pursuit of her this summer... and my group activities. And more than likely, she mentioned my list of questions (my 57 questions). When I say it out loud, it really does sound ridiculous, but at the time, I just wanted to be around Elise any way I could.

When it came to Nikki, I felt like I was auditioning for her; trying to gain her approval as if she was Elise's mother. Her mother would have been easier. I think we all know the approval of a girl's best friend is way more important than that of her mother.

Fortunately, Doug's condition and his drunken babble took the pressure off of me. Sort of.

"That's the last time I listen to my gut," Doug said stuffing his face with Crab Rangoons.

As Doug lamented about the end of his relationship, Elise seemed genuinely sympathetic. Nikki, on the other hand, was more amused than sympathetic. I was somewhere in between. Doug pounded down his beer, belched, then addressed Elise and I.

"I'm sorry I'm ruining your date tonight."

"You're not," Elise said. "Besides, it's not really a date," she added.

She was right of course, but still, hearing her say it out loud was a bit of a punch in the stomach. But I decided it was best to continue her line of thinking.

"Yeah, it's not a date," I said. "More like a non-date, date. We're just hanging out. It's more like a…"

I didn't get to finish my sentence as Doug loudly interrupted, "Shut up already! I'm tired of hearing about this non-date, date, group-date shit! Let's just cut to the chase. Elise, he likes you. Like a lot. Just the other night he told me…"

"Alright, alright, enough," I said cutting him off. "Dude, you're drunk."

"Ya think?" he joked.

Like I said, Nikki was quite amused by Doug's banter. Me, not so much. Doug could tell his observation made us a bit uncomfortable, so he attempted to ease the situation.

"Ya know what? Who am I to be talking about dating anyway? I should just face the facts; I'm not good at the whole dating thing."

Nikki let out a slight laugh and Elise promptly elbowed her.

"It's okay," said Doug. "She's right. Dating and I are laughable. Bottom line is I suck at relationships.

He wasn't completely wrong, but still, I joined Elise in giving the poor guy a sympathetic look.

"There's only one part of the relationship I'm good at," he said.

"The ending?" joked Nikki.

Again, Elise elbowed her.

"No. Well yes," smiled Doug. "But what I'm even better at are the beginnings. You know, the whole *brand new-get to know you* phase? Yup, that's what I'm really good at; the beginnings. Besides, that's the most exciting phase anyway, right Josh?"

Doug was a drunken, babbling fool, but he was kind of right. At this point in my life, I had experienced way more of the beginning, newness stages as opposed to the rest of the relationship phases. There was something to be said about the *getting to know you* phase.

"A toast," he said to me, "to the new car smell!"

I appeased him by clinking his beer. When he polished off the rest of it, he motioned over to Mr. Wong, who was waiting on another table across the way.

By the time Mr. Wong made his way over to us, Doug had his head in his hands lying on the table. Upon seeing this, Mr. Wong's pearly white smile quickly turned to one of concern.

"His girlfriend just dumped him," I informed Mr. Wong.

"Ahhh, he a need some of my Shaolin Punch," smiled Mr. Wong.

"Nooo!" I quickly said. "He definitely does not!"

Mr. Wong began to pat Doug on his back. Slowly, Doug raised his head and pathetically said, "The worse thing is, I still want her back. There's just something about her..."

I prayed that he didn't mention the whole head-tap thing.

Thankfully, he didn't. Mr. Wong continued patting Doug's back and offered his consolement... and words of wisdom.

"Ahh, Mr. Wong understand. It's a like Confucius say: 'Every little thing she does is magic, every little thing just turns you on.'"

Elise, Nikki, and I couldn't help but laugh at Mr. Wong once again using Sting and the Police's lyrics in place of Confucius'. Doug however, was either too drunk or too stupid to catch on. He simply sat there, looking at Mr. Wong in awe.

"Exactly! Exactly, Mr. Wong!" Doug exclaimed.

Again, he patted Doug on his back and said, "Mr. Wong knows your heart will one day soon be filled again with sunshine and happiness."

"Maybe one day," Doug sadly said, "but for now it's just dark clouds and sadness."

Sympathetically, Mr. Wong nodded then said, "It's also like Confucius say: 'There's a little black spot on the sun today. It's the same old thing as yesterday. It's your destiny to be the king of pain. King of pain!'"

Doug grabbed Mr. Wong's hand, looked him straight in the eyes, and said, "Confucius is one smart mother fucker!"

Doug then stood up and gave Mr. Wong a big, drunken hug. How the three of us didn't burst out laughing, I have no idea.

***

We walked the girls to Elise's car in the beach parking lot across the street. Well, we walked, Doug stumbled. With Nikki in the passenger seat and Doug slumped on the curb by the car, I approached Elise.

"Sorry about tonight," I said pointing over to Doug.

"He gonna be okay?" she asked.

"Yeah, he'll be fine," I nodded and changed the subject. "So, August 30th is fast approaching. What am I gonna do with myself when you leave?"

"Somehow I think you'll survive," she said.

"I don't know. I've gotten quite used to seeing you every day this summer."

I should have ended the night with that sweet sentiment, but I didn't.

"You know what, Elise? You're kind of like nicotine… or crack."

I think you can guess the kind of *crazy, what the fuck did you just say* look she shot me.

"Not that I've ever done crack," I clarified. "I just meant you're addictive. I mean, being around you is addictive. Every time I don't see you for a day, I find myself jonesing for you. I totally don't mean that in a sexual way! I just mean, well… I don't really know what I mean except I'm gonna miss you when you leave. It's a total compliment," I pointed out.

"Ummm, thanks?" she said, not knowing what just hit her.

"Well, on that note, I think I'm gonna head home. You guys

all set for a ride?"

I nodded yes. I was tempted to try and explain my whole addictive analogy, but decided it was best to leave well-enough alone. After they drove off, I helped Doug to his feet and led him towards my car.

"Did you just compare her to crack?" Doug slurred.

"Yes. Yes I did," I sighed.

"I fuckin' love you, man," he laughed and put his arm around me.

Luckily for me, the rest of the night was spent on Doug's heartbreak and not my stupid analogies.

Like I said before, Doug is more of a 'play the field' kinda guy as opposed to a serious relationship. But when he does fall for a girl and it ends, his coping methods are not unlike mine. Sort of.

He doesn't really do candles or the incense, but he does like to crank up some depression-session type of music. The big difference being: I like to listen to an array of sad songs, hence my many, many volumes of Depression Session tapes. But Doug usually just picked one or two songs and played them on repeat - for the whole night.

Tonight's duo of choice was "Hey Jealousy" by the Gin Blossoms and "Everything Falls Apart" by Dog's Eye View. Ninety plus minutes of those two songs playing over and over, all the while Doug recounted all the good times they had together. How many good times can one couple have in a two week relationship, you ask? Apparently, a fuckin' shit-ton!

It's nights like this that I realized how my friends must feel when I do the same thing. Except, I might even be more pathetic, because I've spent a whole night (two depression sessions) recounting all the good times I had with a girl I only went out with twice.

21

"THE EXPLODING BOY" – The Cure

I woke up the next morning on a mission. I was determined to ask Elise out on a date. A date, date. A one-on-one date. Unfortunately, I was never able to find the right moment at work to ask her. It was either too busy or there were too many distractions, so I decided to wait until I walked her to her car that night.

There was a big lull between lunch and dinner but that was taken up by a visit from Pete and Michelle. It was their final goodbye visit. They were on their way out of town to start their new life in Florida. I'd like to say it was bittersweet, but the truth was it was more bitter than sweet. I know this sounds selfish of me. This was big and exciting for them;

engaged, moving to a brand new place, starting a new career and life together. I was happy for them. I really was, but I couldn't help but to feel sad. One of my best and longest friends was leaving our hometown. No more spontaneous basketball games, no more late night walkabouts. I know, I know, I'm acting like he was dying or something.

I tried to convince myself that they'd be so homesick that they'd be back to York by Christmas. Sadly for me, I would be wrong.

"So, this is the big goodbye, huh?" I said.

"Yup," Pete said putting his arm around Michelle. "Sorry we didn't get a chance to hang out more the last few nights. The last minute packing was a killer."

"Yeah, I bet. Did you say goodbye to Scott and Doug yet?" I asked.

"Yeah, we went out to lunch earlier with Scott and Lauren. We swung by to see if Doug wanted to go, but he was still in bed."

I nodded and said, "He had a rough night."

"I assumed that when I heard 'Hey Jealousy' on repeat."

All three of us laughed.

"We're really going to miss you guys," Michelle said, and then offered the prerequisite, "Once we get settled, you guys should totally come down and visit."

I also offered the prerequisite, "Definitely. We'll be down there a ton."

It wasn't that I didn't mean it. Of course I meant it. It's

just that everyone always promises to visit or to stay in touch, but for whatever reason, it rarely works out as planned. In the five, that's right FIVE years they would be in Florida, I only got down there once.

Before Pete said his official goodbye, he did offer me something that made the situation more sweet than bitter. He asked if I would be his best man next year at the wedding. Yup, definitely more sweet than bitter.

***

Like I said, I was forced to wait until the end of the night to propose my date question to Elise. As we walked to her car, I started with small talk. And by small talk I mean I checked a couple more easy questions off my list.

By the time we got to her car, my hands were actually sweating. I had done my best throughout the day to rehearse what I was going to say, but now that we were here, the words escaped me.

"Oh, by the way, how's Doug doing?" she asked as she unlocked her door.

"Doug? Oh he'll be fine. He bounces back from these things pretty fast," I said.

Elise started to respond, but I cut her off and blurted out, "I think we should go out. Like one-on-one. No pressure, no expectations."

As soon as I saw her hesitate, I pounced again. "Don't get

me wrong, I've loved our group dates... get-togethers, whatever, but I just think we should go out at least once on our own. I just want to give you a special night before you leave."

Before she could say a word, I continued to pounce and attack.

"I know exactly what you're gonna say. You're gonna say you don't need or deserve a special night, but that's exactly why I wanna do it. The fact that you don't think you're anything special makes you even more special. Just like the fact that you don't think you're cute or funny makes you even more cute and funny, ya know?"

I was relentless with my pouncing and also with my babbling. I decided to finish her off by giving her the slightly pathetic puppy-dog eyes. Whether it was my patheticism or my endearing brown eyes, I could tell her reluctance was starting to crumble. It was as if I was back in the Fun-O-Rama playing Mortal Kombat and the voice on the game was saying, FINISH HIM (her)!

And finish I did.

"Come on Elise, you know you wanna say yes (puppy-dog eyes on full display)."

Although her mouth never actually said yes, her eyes and smile said all I needed to hear.

"Tomorrow night. Five o'clock. I'll pick you up."

Again, her eyes and smile confirmed.

I barely waited for her taillights to fade before I started my arms-in-the-air victory dance. As I drove home that night, two things entered my mind:

1) Excitement - Only 17.5 hours until our date!

2) Pessimism – She had 17.5 long hours to reconsider and come up with an excuse to bail.

Fortunately for me, back in '95 I was still a glass half full kinda guy. Sadly, that wouldn't always be the case.

22

"JUST LIKE HEAVEN" – The Cure

The next day I got out at three, which only left me two hours for my pre-date preparations. I'm not talking about planning what we were going to do, for I'd been working on that all summer. But there were other pre-date preparations that needed to be attended to.

If I was efficient, I could shit, shower, and shave in thirty-three minutes. It took six minutes to get to her house, so that left me an hour and twenty-one minutes for the other stuff.

Other stuff being: A car wash, a full car vacuum, Armor All the dash, and buy a new car-freshener tree. And considering Elise always used watermelon flavored Chapstick, it was a no-brainer which scented tree I'd buy.

The final and perhaps the most crucial pre-date prep work was choosing the perfect mixtape to play in the car. I remembered her answers to question #7; her first and last concert she'd been to. Luckily, I still had plenty of that type of top 40/dance music from my DJ days.

I know what you're thinking, after the car wash and other stuff, there was no way I'd have time to make a mixtape. That's why I stayed up 'til 2am the previous night busting it out. No rookies here!

Not wanting to seem too eager and punctual, I made sure I arrived at her cottage at 5:03 pm. Before I could get out of my car, she exited the house. I immediately knew I was in for it. To steal a word from Freddy, she looked africkinmazing. Her hair was in short tight tails and she was wearing her blue-rimmed glasses. She also had on a blue form-fitting top and white shorts which accented her tanned legs.

I was tempted to rush out and open her door. You know, chivalry and shit, but I thought that might be too over-the-top. Instead, I chose a happy medium. I pushed open her door while still inside my car. I already made sure the mixtape was playing loud enough to hear, but soft enough to talk over. That in itself is an art form.

"Hey," she said getting into my car.

I started with, "Wow! You look amazing! Like totally!"

I immediately chastised myself and told myself to take the eagerness down a few notches. After she blushed and thanked me, I followed it with, "No, seriously, you look super-amazing tonight. Not that you don't normally look amazing but…"

It was at that point I knew the over-eager thing would be a work in progress. A slow work in progress.

Within thirty-eight seconds, she made a comment on how good my car smelled and how she loved watermelon. (Score one for Josh)

"Are you hungry yet for dinner?" I asked.

"I'm actually starving," she said. "It was so busy at work that I didn't get a chance to eat lunch."

"Yeah, it was crazy today. I didn't get a chance to eat either. I was also too nervous to eat."

"Too nervous?" she said.

"Well, yeah. It took me the whole summer to get you to go out with me one-on-one. I just want to make sure everything I have planned tonight goes perfectly."

"Just how many things do you have planned?" she curiously asked.

"Just four things," I said. "With a couple of backup ideas."

"Four things? With backup ideas? Should I be nervous?" she joked.

"Not at all," I said. "You do like Italian food, right?"

"Does Phil like duct tape?" she said with a smile.

"Good," I laughed. "I'd hate to have to dip into my backup ideas so early."

I ended up taking Elise to Mimo's Italian restaurant. It's located at Long Sands, directly across from the beach.

Besides being a great location and romantic, it was BYOB. I brought in a bottle of red wine and was a little surprised that Elise only had one glass. Actually, I never really saw her drink much that whole summer. I, however, drank just enough to take the edge off and calm my nerves. I really did want this night to be perfect.

Surprisingly, dinner went very well. There were rarely any awkward silences, and I actually limited my babbling significantly. I made sure to stay away from any type of relationship questions. She talked about her parents and even shared some funny stories about herself as a kid.

Also, I was pleasantly shocked about her knowledge of the Boston sports teams... all of them. Without me specifically asking, she even answered three of my questions on my list. Yes, I brought my list, which was nearly finished too.

After our very successful semi-romantic dinner, we moved onto Phase Two: York's Wild Kingdom & Amusement Park.

The best way to describe the amusement park is to call it the place that time forgot. The place is promoted as a nostalgic and classic seaside amusement park, which is pretty much just a euphemism for old and rundown. They still had the same rides, the same games, and the same stuffed animal prizes. The only thing that changed over the years were the prices. Despite all of that, you still had to go there at least once every summer.

"I'm surprised we never came here on one of our *work get-togethers*," Elise joked as she put the work get-togethers in air quotes.

"You're making fun of me, aren't you?" I asked.

"A little bit," she smiled. "I'm just kidding. I actually had a lot of fun this summer at the restaurant and on our get-togethers. You're a good activity planner."

"Yeah, yeah," I said as we walked by the Scrambler.

"It's been forever since I've been here," she said. "My grandparents used to take us here when we were younger."

"So you've really been coming here every summer and we've never ran into each other?"

"No. I mostly just came here when I was a kid, and it was usually only for a week or so. Once I became a teenager, I became more interested in spending the summers with my friends back in Vermont. I did come here for two weeks when I was sixteen, but that's only because they let me bring a friend."

"That must have been fun," I said.

"Super-fun," she said. "So fun and crazy that I wasn't offered to bring a friend again. That was the last summer I spent here. I totally regret that now." Sadly, Elise paused. "One week. One week was all my grandparents ever wanted from me, and I chose my friends over that."

"You were just being a typical teenager, Elise."

She just shrugged and looked away. I needed to lighten the mood and change the subject. I stopped walking and pointed down.

"Here. It was right here," I said. "I was ten years old. I got off one of the rides and threw up. Here. I threw up right here. And it was blue because I had eaten blue cotton candy. Yup, I remember."

Although she gave me a disgusted look, I had just successfully changed the subject and lightened the mood.

"What was the ride?" she asked as we continued walking. "Which ride made you sick?"

"The Tilt-A-Whirl," I embarrassingly mumbled under my breath.

"The Tilt-A-Whirl?" You got sick on the Tilt-A-Whirl?" she laughed.

"Yeah, but I don't think it was the regular one. I think it was called the Super-Sonic Tilt-A-Whirl or something. It was fast. Wicked fast. It was one bad-ass ride I tell ya."

She totally wasn't buying my bullshit, but it was nice to see the smile return to her face. There's something to be said about being able to make a girl smile or laugh. Of course, it's even better when it's not *at* you, but sometimes you just got to take what you can get.

Elise gazed around the park then turned to me and said, "I haven't been here in forever, but it wasn't always this..."

"Rundown? Cheesy?" I said. "Yup, always."

"It's weird how when you're a kid, all the rides seemed so shiny and fun. Like that, for instance," she said pointing to the old, rickety rollercoaster.

It wasn't one of those giant high-thrill coasters, but more like a kiddie no-thrill coaster.

"When I was a kid," she continued, "that coaster seemed so scary, but now it seems... well, scary, but for different reasons."

We both cringed watching the coaster careen around a corner as the kids raised their hands and screamed. It was hard to tell if they were screaming out of joy or because they were scared shitless that the track was going to collapse.

Elise looked around at some of the ride attendants and said, "And is it me or does everyone running the rides look like they're on parole or child molesters?"

"You mean when the clown used to touch me in the funhouse, it wasn't part of the ride?" I joked.

Elise laughed out loud. Literally.

We spent the next hour just walking around taking in the sights and sounds. The only ride we went on was the go-carts. Elise beat me. I let her. Maybe. I also tried to win her a giant stuffed panda thingy. I failed. Four times. Well, fourteen times actually. Fuckin' carny games will be the death of me.

We compared notes on all the other amusement parks we've been to. I was jealous that she had been to Cedar Point in Ohio – the rollercoaster capital of the U.S. She had also been to Hershey Park in Pennsylvania. My jealousy quickly turned to shock and sympathy when I learned that she had never been to Disney World, ever. Or Seaworld or Busch Gardens. She'd never even been to Florida period. I made a mental note of that. First date, York's Wild Kingdom, twelve date, Florida and Disney! (Seriously, that's how my mind thinks sometimes).

As the sun began to set, we decided to tackle the miniature golf course, which was tucked in the center of the park. The course, like the park, had seen better days. It was actually a challenging course. Not because it was designed that way, but because it *became* that way.

Take for instance, holes two, four, and seven; all of which had roots from the surrounding trees busting through the well-faded artificial grass putting greens. Also, scattered about the course were oversized and highly kitschy plastic animals.

When we got to the hole with the giant gorilla, I told Elise about the time we almost stole him. It was on one of our off-season walkabouts. It was around 3am and we were a tad bit drunk. Drunk enough that it took more than an effort to climb the tall wooden fence into the park.

Doug had big ideas of taking the gorilla home with us. The bolts holding it in place were pretty rusted so it probably would have been easy to break him free. I actually remember the four of us standing there having a heated debate on the pros and cons of the gorilla snatching.

Pros: 1) It would look cool in one of our houses.

2) It would make for a great story one day.

Cons: 1) It took every ounce of energy for us to scale the fence so how would we do it with a gigantic gorilla?

2) Even if we got it over the fence, wouldn't we look suspicious walking the mile or so back home carrying a giant gorilla?

3) Even if we succeeded with #1 and #2, how would we ever get it through our doorway? The fuckin' thing was like four feet wide. And we couldn't very well put it out on the lawn, the York PD would surely have an APB out on the missing black beast of the jungle. Not to mention, if we put it our yard, someone could easily steal it in the middle of the night. Fuckin' punks!

Needless to say, we left Gus the Gorilla as is and untouched. Well, we might have taken turns mounting Gus in various sexual positions, but I won't completely confirm that. Let's just say, thank God cell phones or social media weren't around then.

After Elise stopped laughing at the vivid imagery I painted of that fateful night, I realized that even though we never actually stole Gus, it still made for a pretty damn good story.

Anyway, when we arrived at the eighteenth hole, I instructed Elise about our guy ritual.

"You guys do what?" she asked.

"We made sure no one was looking then we whale our golf ball over there," I said pointing across the way to the go-cart track.

"You're kidding, right?" she asked.

"Nope," I smiled. "We try and peg someone driving the carts. Doug and I do it all the time."

She still looked skeptical, so I showed her. I set my ball on a flat dirt surface beside the putting green. I carefully scanned the area to make sure no one was looking. When the coast was clear, I whacked the crap out of the ball then put my hand to my ear. When I didn't hear anyone on the track scream out in pain, I turned to Elise and shrugged, "Shit. Nothing. Oh well, your turn."

"No way!" she said. "What if I hit someone?"

"No offense," I laughed, "but if I can't nail someone, I'm sure you won't either. But just do it. It'll be fun."

I took the ball from her hand and placed it on the dirt and then I stepped off to the side.

"Just whack the crap outta it," I said.

Hesitantly, she approached the ball. She gripped her club tightly and as she swung, she closed her eyes. She shanked the ball hard right... as in, *right* into my nuts. She opened her eyes, put her hand to her ear and repeated my phrase.

"Shit. Nothing."

It wasn't until she looked over to see my reaction that she saw me doubled over in excruciating pain.

***

We climbed back into my car; some more gingerly than others. Still nursing my family jewels, I turned the key and started the car. I could tell Elise felt horrible.

"I'm so sorry for hitting you in your... well, you know. There totally needs to be caution tape around me at all times," she said.

I smirked and pushed downward on my stomach and in an exaggerated high-pitch voice I said, "It's okay, they're almost back in place. Don't worry, it shouldn't affect phase three."

"Oh really?" she said with a look.

"I didn't mean phase three was sexual in any nature," I quickly clarified.

We made our way back through Long Sands and into York Harbor. I parked in the semi-secluded Harbor Beach. The sun had set and the nearly full moon was slowly rising over the ocean. The moon, the stars, the ocean in front of us, all contributed to Elise shooting me a nervous look. I knew what she must be thinking, so I was quick to quell her concerns.

"Don't worry, I didn't bring you here to make-out," I said.

"Uh huh," she said and let out a slightly relieved smile. A little *too* relieved for me, but I went with it.

"Now when we go park up at the lighthouse later, that's a different story," I said with a joking wink.

I then grabbed my backpack and motioned her to follow me. Instead of taking the clichéd romantic walk on the beach, I led her up to one of the hidden jewels of York Beach - the Harbor Cliff Walk.

The narrow, and at times rugged path, leads you along the cliffs overlooking York Harbor. The breathtaking ocean views were much more visible and better during the day, not to mention, the path itself was 100% safer in daylight as well.

But I figured with the moon as full as it was, it would make for a unique and memorable walk.

"Have you ever been out on the Cliff Walk?" I asked.

Slowly and a little scared, she shook her head no.

"I didn't even know this existed. Is this like really a cliff walk? As in, we walk on cliffs? Cliffs high above the ocean?"

"Yup," I said.

"Are we supposed to be up here after sunset?" she asked.

"Probably not," I said.

"How are we supposed to see? It's so dark…"

She stopped when she saw me pull two flashlights out of my backpack.

"I come prepared," I said handing her a flashlight.

"It's probably gonna be pretty cold up along the cliffs, huh?" she said rubbing her hands on her bare arms.

"Probably," I said pulling out a sweatshirt for her to wear. "Told you, I come prepared."

***

After we walked for a bit, we climbed out onto a gigantic rock and sat and talked, and to my surprise, she did most of the talking, or I should say, most of the asking. She had her own questions for me. She knew I was upset yesterday regarding the departure of Pete and Michelle. Elise not only asked how I was doing, but asked about their story; how long had I known them, etc.

I told her Michelle used to be a summer girl and she met Pete lifeguarding. I told Elise some of the silly stories about the first summer they met, and I even told her about when Pete and I first met way back in middle school.

I have to admit, it was a little cathartic recounting old stories about all of us friends, and I was appreciative of Elise allowing me to do so. Her next question was a bit more depressing for me.

"Have you ever been close?" she asked. "To marriage, I mean."

"Oh, I see how it goes," I joked. "I'm not allowed to ask you relationship questions, but you can ask me?"

She was quick with an apology.

"You're right. I totally don't have the right to ask you that."

"Relax, Elise. I'm just kidding. And no, I have never been close to marriage or even engagement."

That simple statement got me thinking. Part of me was more than okay with the fact I wasn't married or even engaged yet. I didn't have a penny to my name, a real job, or even a career path carved out yet. My proverbial ducks were certainly not in a row.

But there was another part of me that was depressed; not about the duck thing, although that was pretty depressing in itself. I guess what really saddened me was I had never, ever come close to the marriage/engagement thing.

I briefly went into detail about some of my minor relationships, including my fifth grade relationship with Leah Gagnon. It wasn't much of a story considering it only lasted four and a half recesses. I even went into detail about Jane and how it always seemed to be a case of bad timing.

"Well, maybe one day the timing will be right," Elise sympathetically said.

"It is what it is," I shrugged. "I guess I'm kind of like Doug, I'm better at the beginnings rather than the actual relationship. It's a good thing the beginnings are the best part," I joked.

The joke was my way of saving face from my lack of any real relationship success. Little did I know, my silly joke would come back to bite me in the ass bigtime in the days to come.

The next few minutes were spent in silence with both of us just taking in the scenic beauty of the bright moon reflecting off the ocean. Combine that with the sounds of the waves lapping far below us, and the foghorn off in the distance... it was perfect.

Of course, what truly made the moment perfect was the next question out of Elise's mouth. It was perhaps one of my most favorite questions ever, and I was pissed I hadn't included it on my fifty-seven question list. My *what are your top 3 fave bands* question was similar, but the way she worded her question was different and perfect!

"So, I have another question for you," she said.

"You have your own question list going, don't you?" I smiled.

She rolled her eyes and continued, "If you were to make a mixtape of songs that best described you, what would it consist of?"

My jaw dropped open. This was the best question ever. My *what are your top 3 fave bands* question was so generic... and boring... and limiting. Her question was so much cooler. My mind raced with possibilities. She could tell my musical wheels were turning.

"You don't have to answer it now," she laughed. "You can get back to me before I leave next week," she smiled.

I was relieved. An answer like that needed some serious time and consideration. As we sat there on the rock, my brain was like a musical pinball machine. There were bells, and whistles, and flashing lights as my silver pinball ricocheted off one great song after another. Great fuckin' question, I thought.

I literally could have sat there all night with her, but as I looked at my watch, I knew we had to get going.

"We should head out," I said. "Phase four awaits."

"Not that I'm complaining, but how many phases do you have again?"

"Just four," I said as I led her back down the cliff walk and to my car.

***

So far, everything was going better than planned. She even got a good laugh at one of the musical selections on my mixtape playing in my car. I timed it perfectly. About halfway to phase four, the band Enigma started playing. In case you don't know or remember, Enigma was this atmospheric dance-beat type music with Gregorian monk chants.

As soon as it came on, I cranked it up and looked over at her and said, "Feel free to sing along there, choir girl."

She just shook her head, smiled, and said, "Phase four better not involve me doing karaoke."

"Nah. What I have in store is much, much better," I said.

By the time we arrived at the Short Sands parking lot, I knew her curiosity was piqued. Even more so when we headed towards the Fun-O-Rama.

"Phase four is the Fun-O-Rama?" she asked.

"Nope," I said as we headed up the large wooden stairs and into the arcade.

The place was just getting ready to close for the night, which was fine because I was just using it as a short cut. We walked straight through the arcade and out its back door. Once outside, we headed down the dark side street until we reached the York Beach Cinema. The marquee out front read: "Clueless" Just as we approached, there were droves of people exiting the theater.

"Um, is this phase four?" Elise hesitantly whispered.

I nodded my head yes.

"Um, you do know that was the last showing of the night, right?"

"Really?" I said with a fake, pretend concern. "Hmmm, let's go check." I motioned her to follow me inside.

By the time we entered the lobby, the place was void of all customers. The concession counter was closed and most of the lights were off. With my trusty backpack in tow, I headed into the theater.

"Where are you going?" she asked.

"I'm pretty sure there's another showing," I said. My smile was a dead give-away that something was up my sleeve.

The inside of the theater had that musty smell of nostalgia. It also smelled of buttered popcorn, sweaty teenagers, and a hint of sun tan lotion. I let Elise choose our seats.

"I can't believe you're having them do an extra showing of 'Clueless' just for us."

I was bursting at the seams. She had no idea what she was in for. Luckily, I didn't have to burst for long, the lights dimmed and the projector came on. Rather than looking at the screen, my eyes were focused on what Elise's reaction would be in 3...2...1... and there it was; her jaw dropped and the biggest smile came over her face.

There, on the screen, was the opening credits to "The Master of the Flying Guillotine."

"Shut up," she said turning towards me. "How did you do this?"

"Enjoy the movie," I winked. "I'll tell you after."

The truth was, like all good plans, I had an inside connection. This particular connection was Wild Willy. He was about five years older than me, but we had a lot of mutual friends. By day, he could be found beach bummin' it down at Long Sands; sun-tanning, smoking, and surfing. By night, he was the main man at the cinema. I actually approached him at the beginning of the summer when I found out what kind of movies Elise liked. Yup, even back then I was laying the groundwork just in case she ever said yes to a date.

I did think it would have been much sooner than now, but whatever. Anyway, I told Wild Willy about Elise's cheesy Kung Fu movie obsession, and as luck would have it, he knew a guy who knew a guy. And that guy not only ran the Strand Theater up in Rockland, Maine, but he was known to do a few Kung Fu marathons throughout the year. And as double luck would have it, one of the movies he had was "The Master of the Flying Guillotine."

And yes, it would have been extremely embarrassing to have laid all the groundwork for this if Elise would have ended up saying no. The look on her face as the movie played made it totally worth the risk.

I counted at least eight times that she turned to me and said, "I can't believe you did this."

On the third time, I decided to take it up a notch.

"Are hungry or thirsty?" I asked.

"You had them open the concession stand just for us too?"

"Nope. I did one better," I said as I pulled a can of Diet Coke from my backpack. "Diet Coke. From the can. Rumor has it, it tastes better from the can."

She smiled and shook her head, and before she could say anything, I said, "And I know these probably don't go well together, but I also got you this." I pulled out a box of Cap'n Crunch. "With crunchberries," I pointed out.

She thought I was insane and utterly ridiculous, but it didn't matter as I watched her excitedly crack open her soda and then dig into the cereal. Note to self: Cap'n Crunch is way, way louder than popcorn. It was a good thing this wasn't the type of movie that you really needed to hear what was being said.

When the movie ended, I thanked Wild Willy and introduced him to Elise. Fun fact: Wild Willy's favorite drink was Diet Pepsi... also from the can.

As soon as our feet hit the sidewalk outside, she turned to me and said again, "I can't believe you did this. There's no way you could have planned this since you asked me out yesterday?"

As we walked back towards my car, I explained the whole crazy process of my master plan. When we got to my car, I took a chance and asked, "Do you wanna keep walking?"

I braced myself for her to say *Thanks, but I really should get going,* but she didn't. instead, she nodded and said, "Sure."

We continued up the boardwalk along Short Sands. By now it was nearly 1am, and besides some distant laughter coming from the darkened beach, we were the only ones on the sidewalk.

"I told you it was a cool movie, didn't I?" she smiled.

"Yeah, I'm surprised it never won any awards," I joked.

With the ocean on our left and Ellis Park on our right, we walked up the slight hill to where Short Sands ended. There, we turned around and made our way back. Not much was spoken on the return walk. Once again, it wasn't an uncomfortable silence. I think we were both just enjoying the cool salt air and the sound of the waves breaking in the distance.

What happened next completely and totally caught me off guard. No, she didn't throw me on the sand and jump my bones. I think anyone who's actually done that knows it's overrated. Weeks later you're still digging sand out of cracks and crevices you didn't even now you had.

Anyway, like I said, she didn't jump my bones in the sand. I know I could get my man card revoked for saying this, but what she did next was even better than sand sex.

We walked past the fenced-in playground, and she asked if I wanted to go in. I happily agreed and followed her in and sat next to her on the swings. No, there was no swing sex either.

After a few minutes of slow, lazy swinging, it happened.

Elise let her guard down and let me in. It wasn't like her walls came a crumbling down, but a few bricks definitely fell out, and she allowed me to see into her a little bit more.

"My longest relationship was back in high school. A year and a half. Keith Bergeron. He was one of the good ones, ya know? Which was ironic seeing as most of the guys at my school were total jerks and dirt bags.

My absolute best friend in the world was Holly Lockwin. She was one of the sweetest and most real people you'll ever meet. We'd been friends since elementary school. About halfway through our senior year, Derek McAllister had this huge party. His parents were gone for the week and it was billed as the biggest party of the year. It definitely lived up to it. It seemed like the whole school was there.

Keith worked at a restaurant a few towns over and wouldn't be there until late. Holly was stuck at home, sick in bed with strep, so I went with other friends. I was kind of a wild child back then. Well, maybe not so much wild, but let's just say I had a hard time monitoring my alcohol intake. Keith was always my babysitter at parties, making sure I didn't get too messed up. He hated when I got too drunk. He said I'd turn into a huge, obnoxious bitch."

I found it hard to picture shy, quiet Elise as ever being an obnoxious bitch, but I have seen some pretty scary transformations of people when they drink.

"Unfortunately, he wasn't there to babysit me that night and neither was Holly. I don't know what got into me, but I started drinking anything and everything. I remember playing that card game *Asshole* with Holly's boyfriend Zach and a bunch of others. The rest of the night was a hazy blur, at best. The last thing I remembered was being in the living room 'Vogue-ing' to Madonna. It wasn't until the next morning I found out what I did."

Elise sadly paused, and I forced my creaking swing to a full halt. My heart felt for her. I knew exactly what must have happened. I was tempted to tell her she didn't have to go on, but instead, I just sat quietly. When she regained her composure, she continued her story.

"Apparently, my boyfriend showed up after midnight and went looking for me. Not only did he find me in bed with my best friend's boyfriend, he found us... in the act. I didn't remember a thing," she said as a tear ran down her cheek.

"Oh, Elise, I'm so sorry," was all I could say.

"It was my own fault. I deserved the consequences. Still to this day, neither one will talk to me. I can't say I blame them. I totally screwed up."

I had absolutely no idea what to say to her, so I said nothing. Neither of us said anything. Part of me was happy that she trusted me enough to let me in to see a piece of her life; a piece she had obviously kept well-guarded. But I couldn't help but wonder if this sad and quiet moment was what she'd remember about our date.

***

As I pulled into her driveway, I was determined not to let the date end on a sour note. Even if that meant doing my babbling thing.

"Just because you made a stupid mistake in high school, it doesn't define who you are. We've all done dumb things that we regret. You're not a bad person, Elise. You're not."

I could tell she wasn't buying what I was selling.

"I don't think you give yourself enough credit, Elise. And I certainly don't think you realize just how many great qualities you actually have. As a matter of fact, do you know what you're like?

She forced a slight smirk and said, "Like crack?"

"Ha ha," I smiled. "Touche. No, not crack. You're like a greatest hits record... album... CD, whatever."

Her familiar *What are you talking about?* look made an appearance.

"That's right," I insisted. "You're like a personality greatest hits record. Most people's personality album might produce one big hit, maybe. If they're lucky, maybe a few top ten hits, but usually the rest of their album is average at best. But with you, Elise, the frickin' hits keep coming!"

I went on to list all of her many amazing personality traits. She blushed after each one.

"So there! You're definitely a personality greatest hits record! Oh, and you're funny too, but not in a trying to be funny way, which makes you even funnier. Yup. Funny is your hidden bonus track."

She offered a smile then put her hand on the door handle. I panicked and continued to babble, and I went down a babbling road that maybe I shouldn't have.

"Listen, I know you're leaving next week and all, but I think it'd be nice if we stayed in touch. Actually, it would be great if we stayed in more than in touch. I guess what I'm trying to say is I don't want this summer to end... for us to end. Not that there's an us yet, but I was kinda hoping there could be. Vermont isn't that far. Maybe I could come see you on weekends, or you could come back down here to visit. I'm not sure if you've ever seen the Nubble Lighthouse all lit up at Christmas, but it's pretty cool. Not that I'm saying we should spend Christmas together, but..."

What was I saying? Even my babbling was babbling. I could tell she was speechless and uncomfortable. Very uncomfortable.

"Umm, I don't know... we'll see," she quietly said.

Most would be disheartened by her comment, or her lack of comment, but my inner Jim Carrey (Lloyd Christmas) voice kept telling me, *"So you're saying there's a chance."*

"Well, I should head in. My nana is probably waiting up for me. Thanks for tonight. It was nice."

I was shooting for 'amazing' or 'unbelievably cool', but I'd have to settle for nice. I know the date didn't involve a romp in the sand or even a head tap or whatever. Hell, it didn't even involve a goodnight kiss. But as I drove home that night, I couldn't help feel it was a huge success. Well, everything except my final babbling session.

I made a mental note to clarify my comments to her tomorrow at work. It took a whole summer for her to go on a date with me, and here I am trying to make visitation/relationship plans with her this winter. Fuckin' idiot.

23

"ACHIN' TO BE" – The Replacements

Like most things in my life, Elise's last day didn't go as planned. It was another busy day at the restaurant, so I didn't really have a chance to talk to her; like really talk. Freddy was in extra rare form that day. Not only was he was singing and dancing up a storm, he kept reminding everyone about his huge end of the summer party on Sunday night.

The few times I did cross paths with Elise, it became more and more obvious that something was up, that something was different. I kept getting this uncomfortable, nervous vibe from her. It definitely seemed like she was purposely avoiding me.

Naturally, doubts started to fill my mind. Did she not have as good of a time last night as I thought? Was it my whole spiel about wanting us to see each other this winter? Did I really have to suggest she come up around Christmas because the fuckin' Nubble Lighthouse looked cool all lit up? Did I move too fast and scare her off? Fuck, fuck, fuck! My head was spinning, so I decided to confront her.

"Color me paranoid, but you're not avoiding me, are you?" I asked half- jokingly.

"Umm, no," she said, not making eye contact. "It's just been a busy day, that's all."

"Oh, ok. Hey, I was thinking we should all go out for drinks tonight in honor of your last night at work."

Her reluctance was immediately evident.

"Umm, thanks, but I can't. I promised my grandmother I'd spend as much time with her before I leave on Monday. And I still have to start packing too."

I knew she wasn't going home tonight to pack. And the chances of her grandmother being awake for some quality time later tonight was pretty slim. I didn't push it though. I played it cool.

"Oh, ok. Well, I guess I'll just have to take full advantage of our final walk to your car then. It'll give me a chance to clarify some of my babble from last night."

She gave me a polite smile then made her way back to her customers. As you can probably guess, I never got the chance to walk her to her car that night. She ducked out before I was finished balancing the register draw in the office.

I was tempted to rush home and call her up at her cottage, but I didn't. I knew I'd have one more chance to talk to her before she left on Monday. That chance would be Freddy's big party on Sunday night.

As shitty as I felt about Elise bailing on our walk that night, that was no comparison to how I'd feel on Sunday night.

24

"SO CRUEL" – U2

By the time Sunday night rolled around, I was certainly not in the mood to go to Freddy's big party. I only attended because I promised him I would go. Also, I knew Elise would probably be there. I just needed to talk to her face to face. There was no way I wanted the summer to end with things being left unsaid or unclarified.

Freddy's parents owned a ginormous house up by the Nubble Lighthouse. The fact that his parents were as rich as they were, yet Freddy still worked his ass off all summer, said a lot about Freddy as a person.

He always told me his end of the summer bashes were a not-to-miss event. And by the amount of cars lining the side streets, he was right. Despite claiming to still be heartbroken, I dragged Doug with me to the party.

"Why are we here again?" Doug asked.

"Because I promised Freddy I'd come."

"Your chick is gonna be here, isn't she?" he asked.

"Maybe," I shrugged.

"You have a big speech planned out, don't you?" Doug asked.

"No. It's not that big. I just want to tell her I had a great time the other night."

"And?"

"And that I had a great time working with her this summer."

"And?" he asked again.

"And it would be nice if we stayed in contact," I said. Doug's look replaced the word *and*. I sighed and continued, "And maybe we can keep our options open for something more in the future. Why, is that bad?"

Doug shrugged then simply said, "Probably a step up from comparing her to crack."

I knew I was never living that one down.

"Okay, Romeo, let's do this," said Doug. "But I gotta warn you, I'm still not feeling very social. This whole breakup thing still stings. It could be quite a while until I get my mojo back. So don't be surprised if I bail early."

No sooner did he say this, we watched two cute, young girls get out of a car ahead of us. Both were made-up and wearing belly shirts and mini-skirts. Doug's eyes widened. Needless to say, his mojo had returned.

As he stared mesmerized, one of the girls accidentally dropped her purse, scattering its contents on the road. Doug's eyes widened even more when her black thong was revealed.

"We're definitely staying," he said as he rushed over to help her. "Here, let me help you with that."

"Aww, thanks," she said.

"I'm Doug," he said, not even attempting to pretend not to be staring at her cleavage.

"I'm Abby," she smiled, not even attempting to be offended by his cleavage stare. "We heard this would be the hottest party all summer."

"Well, what are we waiting for?" he said offering his arms to escort the girls.

And just like that, they both grabbed an arm, and they were off. Looks like I'm on my own, I thought as I headed up the long walkway to the house. Before I even got to the large front porch, Freddy rushed out of the house to greet me. It was immediately obvious he was already well-lit.

"Oh my God, Joshua! You came!" he said as he gave me a bear hug. Well, more like a teddy bear hug.

"There's a stocked bar in the house and there's plenty of beer in the fridge. And we've got Jell-O shots galore! One for each color of the rainbow," he proudly smiled.

Freddy's boyfriend, Steve exited the house and exclaimed,

"Yayyy, Freddy's boss is here!"

As he reached out to shake my hand, I could tell he was equally as shit-faced as Freddy.

"No boss tonight," I said. "Just a friend."

"Aww. Youuuuu," Freddy slurred, pointing at me.

Steve put his arm around Freddy, and as they stood side by side, they both started to sway. This wasn't the type of swaying caused by "Careless Whisper" being played. It was simply caused by both of them being drunk as skunks.

As I watched them sway, I asked, "Exactly how many Jell-O shots have you two had already?"

They both looked at each other and did some random counting thing on their fingers. Freddy then looked at me and smiled, "Three rainbows."

While Freddy and Steve giggled uncontrollably, I just turned and started to head towards the house. Before I got up the first step, Freddy grabbed my arm.

"Wait!" he yelled.

"Yes?" I said turning to face him.

"Umm, I swear I didn't invite him, but..."

"Invite who?" I asked.

"Chad and one of his friends are here."

I couldn't help but laugh. I hadn't thought about Mr. Murphy's idiot grandson since I fired him last month.

"It's fine, Freddy," I reassured. "It's a big house. I'm sure we can avoid each other." I turned and headed towards the front door. I only made it two steps before I felt Freddy grab my arm again.

"Wait!" he repeated.

"Yes Freddy?" I asked a little amused.

"Umm, Elise is here."

"Okay, thanks," I smiled.

"And she's a little... well, a lot drunk," Freddy said. "And not on the rainbow either. She went straight for the pot of gold."

I gave Freddy and Steve a puzzled look.

"As in Goldschlager," Freddy exclaimed.

This caught me off guard. I hadn't seen Elise have more than one drink all summer.

"I'm sure she's just letting loose because it's the end of summer," I said as I turned and continued towards the door.

"Wait," Freddy meekly said.

"What now?"

"She's kind of sort of hanging out with Chad."

I immediately felt sick to my stomach. I was hoping at any moment, Freddy would burst out giggling and say, 'Just kidding!' But he didn't. Not at all. Now if I was smart, I would have just turned around and went home, avoiding the whole situation. Who wants to put themselves in a situation where you're watching the girl you like get drunk with a giant asshole? Especially when the giant asshole is one of your arch enemies. It'd be like Superman watching Lois Lane flirt and get drunk with Lex Luther.

I should have turned and went home, but I didn't. I wasn't

smart. Not at all. I entered the party.

You would think with all the rooms in Freddy's house, I could have easily avoided them. But for some stupid, pathetic reason, I found myself standing in the living room doorway watching Elise and Chad laughing on the couch with his fuckin' arm around her. On the opposite side of the room sat Nikki and some dude.

"She's totally out of control."

I turned around to see Megan, Phil, and Phil's girlfriend, Marissa standing there.

"I tried to talk to her earlier," continued Megan, "but she pretty much just laughed me off. What the fuck is she thinking hanging out with him anyway?"

All I could do was shrug. That sick feeling in my stomach was growing by the moment.

"If you want," said Phil, "I can duct tape him to a tree and cover his balls with peanut butter. I'm sure the squirrels would have a field day."

I couldn't even crack a smile at Phil's attempt to lighten the mood. I was too busy debating whether I should go over and say something to Elise. Once again, the smart thing would be to just leave her alone and say nothing. The smart thing would be to go tell Doug I'm leaving.

And once again, I proved I wasn't smart. At all.

I watched Chad get up and head into the kitchen, leaving Elise alone on the couch. She was so drunk she could barely sit up straight. I had to say something to her. I had to.

While reaching for her Goldschlager, she drunkenly knocked it over. I picked up the bottle as the few people standing by us just laughed at her. She reached her hand out for the bottle, but I pulled it away.

"I think you've had enough, don't you?" I said.

"Who are you, my dad?" she huffed.

"No," I quietly said. "Maybe we should go outside and get you some fresh air?" I suggested.

"Awww, you wanna walk me to my car? For old time's sake?" She laughed and turned to the people next to us. "I had to put up with this guy, AKA my BOSS, walking me to my car every night after work this summer."

All I could do was shake my head at her.

"What? You disappointed in me?" she slurred.

"No," I quietly answered. "This isn't the real you."

"Pfft, maybe it is! Maybe I'm not as cute and perfect as you think?"

As everyone stood there staring at us, I literally had no idea what to say. This was a first for me and she knew it.

"Don't tell me the king of babble is speechless?" she laughed. "What? Ya run outta questions on your list for me?"

I felt the knife start to twist in me as she addressed the group of people next to us.

"He wrote down questions for me. Fifty-seven stupid questions! It was his way of *getting to know me better*. Because after all, the whole 'newness-getting-to-know-you' stage is the best part, right? Right?"

The knife twisted deeper as uneasy and uncomfortable looks filled the bystanders' faces.

"Well, I pretty much answered them all," she said, "so I guess you'll have to find another chick to get that new car smell from!"

As if it couldn't get any worse, Chad reentered and took full advantage of the situation.

"Hey Elise, wanna go upstairs?" he said holding up a bottle of Jagermeister.

By now, Megan and Phil had joined me by my side.

"Don't go with him," Megan pleaded.

Elise looked at Megan and then to me. I could see in her eyes just how loaded she was. I wanted to reach out for her; rescue her from what was sure to be a giant mistake. But I didn't. Not only were my legs frozen, but words failed to escape my mouth.

I watched as Chad helped her to her feet and led her out of the room. Chad's smug fuckin' smile burned right through me as they left. It was only after they had completely left the room, that my legs were free to move. I was stone-cold sober, yet I felt as numb and dizzy as if I'd been drinking Jack-n-Coke all day.

It was also as if I blacked out, because the next thing I knew, I was sitting in an Adirondack chair in Freddy's backyard. Their yard was set directly on a cliff overlooking the Atlantic.

Even with the full moon shimmering its light across the

waves, the scenic beauty was completely lost on me. I pounded down the rest of my beer; a beer which I don't even remember getting.

"Hey, you okay?" asked a voice from behind me.

I turned to see Megan, Phil, and Freddy. I nodded my head, but my insincerity was obvious. I could tell they had no idea what to say to me. It was Phil who finally broke the silence in Phil-style.

"Man, she really destroyed you in there, huh?"

Both Megan and Freddy smacked him.

"No, he's right," I said. "She totally destroyed me in there."

"She's just drunk," added Freddy. "She didn't really mean it, Joshua."

"There's always more than an ounce of truth in someone's drunken babble," I said.

"Freddy is right," began Megan. "She didn't mean those things. She's just sabotaging. She's ending things badly first, rather than things to end badly for her. I do it all the time."

"How so?" I asked.

"Most of the guys I go out with are assholes," she began, "but on the rare occasion I go out with a guy who treats me like gold, I totally don't know how to handle it. Not because I don't want to be treated like gold, but because I somehow know it won't last. So rather than wait for the other shoe to fall, I end up sabotaging the relationship. I know it's gonna end eventually, so it might as well be on my terms."

"And you guys think I'm screwed up?" said Phil.

"I'm not saying it's not screwed up," said Megan, "I'm just saying I do it all the time, and Elise is doing the same."

"I think you need some of my famous Jell-O shots," announced Freddy.

"Thanks, but I think I'm just gonna go find Doug and head home."

***

I made my way back into the house and did a quick scan for Doug. I was about to give up, when I heard his laugh come from upstairs. I went up and found him standing at the end of the hallway laughing and flirting with that Abby chick.

We made eye contact and I motioned to him that I was leaving and asked if he was all set. He motioned back a more-than-eager thumbs up. I knew he had no clue what happened with me and Elise earlier. If he had, he would have definitely put his flirting on hold. Even in the throes of seduction, the old cliché, 'bros before hoes' rang true. And no, I'm not saying Abby was a ho. I'm not saying she wasn't one either.

Bottom line, if Doug knew what had happened, he would have been in consolement mode rather than hookup mode. Of course, the day next day he would have made me feel guilty about ruining his chances of getting laid.

Before I could turn around to leave, I heard a voice yell up the stairs.

"Yo, Chad, did you tap that ass yet or what?"

I turned to see Chad exiting one of the bedrooms as his friend walked up the stairs. Chad didn't see me as he addressed his friend.

"Fuck no! She's too fuckin' drunk. She's in the bathroom with her friend, puking her guts out."

"Aw, you're not gonna volunteer to hold her hair back for her?" laughed Chad's friend.

"Fuck that shit! The only time I'll be holding her hair back is when she's sucking my cock."

As the two dickheads laughed, Nikki stepped out of the bathroom. She glared at Chad then she caught my eye over his shoulder. Chad turned around to see what she was looking at and that's when it happened: I became a fighter and not a lover.

Without even knowing what I was doing, I clenched my fist and clocked Chad dead in his smug little face. Blood shot from his nose as he hit the ground like a sack of potatoes.

'Take that, you Rob Lowe looking mother fucker!' is what I should have said, but I was still in shock for punching someone in the nose... hard... hard enough for blood.

Chad's friend rushed up the stairs, but stopped short of doing anything. I'd like to think he was scared that I was gonna Mike Tyson his face too, but I think he really stood down because Doug had appeared by my side.

Doug and I ended up helping Nikki get Elise into her car.

Barely coherent, Elise murmured, "I want to go home."

"Shhh, sweetie, we're heading home now," said Nikki as we placed Elise in the passenger seat.

"You okay to drive?" I asked.

Nikki nodded then said, "Don't read too much into her comments tonight. It's been a long time since I've seen her like this."

"It's nice to know I drove her to get shit-faced," I said sarcastically.

"It's not you, Josh. She's had a rough past when it comes to guys."

"Yeah, I know," I said. "She told me about her high school boyfriend."

Nikki looked at me puzzled. "Um, I'm not sure about that. She never mentioned anything to me about her high school days, but I do know she's had her share of heartbreaks in college."

Part of me was touched that Elise had shared something personal with me, something she hadn't even shared with her friend. But after Nikki's college reference, I knew there was much, much more behind Elise's wall, and I couldn't help but think, I might not ever find out. As much as I wanted to pry more information out of Nikki, I didn't. I just nodded and motioned for her to get Elise home.

25

"A LETTER TO ELISE" – The Cure

After they drove away, Doug and I walked to my car and headed home ourselves. Not a word was spoken on our ride. It wasn't until we exited the car that Doug said something.

"Do ya wanna go for a walkabout?" he asked.

"No thanks," I said.

We entered our apartment and Doug made his way over to my vast music collection.

"Which one do you want?" he said pointing to my Depression Session mixes.

I appreciated his gesture, but I wasn't even in the mood for music; sad music or otherwise. I just wanted to go to bed and try to forget this night ever happened.

Within minutes of me shutting my bedroom door and falling on my bed, I heard Doug crack open not one but two beers. The next thing I knew, our apartment was filled with Radiohead's "Fake Plastic Trees" (Depression Session #7, by the way).

And like a rat drawn to the Pied Piper, I dragged my ass into the living room where a cold beer and sad music awaited me.

When the song faded out, Doug turned to me and said, "You do realize you totally ruined my chances of getting laid tonight, right?"

I looked blankly at Doug then joined him in letting out a laugh. The situation sucked, sucked beyond words, but for the moment anyway, it was nice to have one of my best friends there to commiserate with.

It was somewhere during Depression Session #8 that Doug passed out. So there I was, 2am, wide awake, and thinking. Bad combinations. I couldn't help replaying the night; replaying the whole summer. Did Elise really think I was only after the new car smell from her? Did she really think my questions were stupid? Was Megan right? Was Elise just scared and sabotaging?

My heart and my glass-half-empty mind couldn't seem to agree with each other. The only thing they agreed on was I needed to set Elise straight before she left town. I also needed to find out how she truly felt about me. I needed to come up with the perfect words and say them to her face-to-face in the morning.

It was at that point I started to overthink. What if I started to babble uncontrollably? What if what I was trying to say came out all wrong? And was it really fair to put her on the spot with how she really felt about me?

Ultimately, I decided against the whole face-to-face confrontation. That left only one option: a letter. Not only was I the king of the mixtape, but I was also known to write a letter or ten in my lifetime.

Ironically, this would be my last pen and paper letter I would ever write to a girl. Technology played more into this than anything. Pen and paper letters would be replaced by emails and eventually texts. And yes, I would also have my share of emails and texts… long, long texts.

I grabbed my pad of paper and my lucky pen then hit the stop button on my tape player. I decided to switch formats and use my new CD player. I put in the "Wish" CD by The Cure. I figured it was only appropriate while I wrote a letter to Elise to have the actual "A Letter To Elise" song playing on repeat in the background. Don't judge.

The words actually flowed easily and quickly onto the paper. When I finished, I neatly folded it and sealed it an envelope labeled *A Letter to Elise*. Again, don't judge.

As I sat there looking at my huge music collection (mostly tapes still), I recalled the question Elise had asked me on our 'date': "*If you were to make one mixtape of songs that best represented you, what would it consist of?*"

After our date, I remembered going home and jotting down about twenty songs on a piece of paper. I never got the chance to show her that list, I thought.

Hmmmm. I think you know where I'm going with this, don't you?

So, as the clock struck 4am, not only did I have a letter written, but I had a mixtape made as well. Not only would this be the last pen and paper letter I'd write to a girl, this would be my last mixtape I'd ever make as well. Like I said, technology would change and mixtapes would become mix CDs.

I suppose I could have gotten a little sleep and dropped them off to her in the morning, but being the impulsive, non-patient type, I decided there was no time like the present. I made sure to be extra quiet leaving the apartment. I didn't want to wake up Doug. Partly out of consideration, but mostly because I didn't want him to give me shit.

And before you roll your eyes at me, NO, I didn't knock on her door at four in the morning. I'm not that much of an impulsive idiot. Instead, I simply placed the letter and tape on the windshield of her blue Honda Accord and then I drove back home. It was now in her hands whether she wanted to come talk to me and say goodbye face to face.

Well, in case you were wondering, here's the letter.

Elise,

   I decided to write you a letter because I tend to babble less when I write.

I'm still not sure what the hell happened last night. And I'm still not sure if what you said to me was how you really feel or not. My heart tells me it's not, but my eyes and ears told me something different. Whether that's how you really feel or not, let me make it crystal clear how I feel – just so there are no doubts.

You need to know I meant everything I said to you this summer. You know, like about how sweet, and smart, and how funny you are. And easy on the eyes too. Definitely easy on the eyes. And those glasses you wear sometimes totally drive me crazy. Not crazy bad but crazy good. Anyway, I meant all those things as compliments, as facts. They were NOT pickup lines, or me just trying to get in your pants, or to bang you, or whatever. Wow, so much for babbling less in a letter.

I loved that you were able to open up to me about what happened to you in high school. I know it took a lot to let me behind your wall. It's obvious that you've been hurt badly and that's why you're so protective. It's also obvious that there are many, many more things you have hidden behind there as well. You might not ever let me or anyone else behind there, but you need to know I tried. I tried my very best to tear those walls down this summer. And it had nothing to do with that new car smell or whatever. I just wanted to get to know the real you.

I'd like to think we were starting to build something special, but after last night I don't know. I would love it if you could stop by work to say goodbye to me in person... and maybe tell me exactly how you really feel.

Josh

PS: That 5 minute walk to your car at night? You know, the one you had to 'put up with'? That 5 minute walk was the best part of my day.

26

"THE MOUTAINS WIN AGAIN" – Blues Traveler

The next day at work was torture. Pure torture. First of all, I had to deal with my whole staff going above and beyond being nice to me. It was like a giant pity party, and while I appreciated their efforts, I think I liked it better when the place was an out-of-control shit show. And I'm not going to lie, I constantly found myself eyeing the front door in hopes of Elise showing her face.

I had these grandiose thoughts of her not only coming in to apologize, but her telling me how much she actually liked me, and how she also wanted to stay in touch... in close touch. I know, I know, me and my actively pathetic imagination.

Needless to say, she never showed her face at the restaurant again. This led my brain to wonder: Did she get the tape and letter? If so, did she listen to it? Did she read the letter? Then I thought: What if a huge gust of wind blew them off her windshield? Or what if some early morning walker stole them? Shit! I should have just knocked on her door and handed them to her in person. Better yet, maybe I shouldn't have written the letter. Maybe I should have just said it to her face. Like I said, actively pathetic imagination.

After I turned down everyone's offer to hang out after work, I found myself sitting there alone in the darkened restaurant. Color me nostalgic, or just a glutton for punishment, but I decided to walk to the parking lot where Elise used to park; where I used to walk her every night after work. Is it just me or are there others who force themselves down memory lane, knowing it'll only make you more depressed?

After walking through the parking lot, I headed down to the beach and retraced the steps we took after the movie; right down to sitting on the swings in the playground. And because I was truly a glutton for punishment, instead of driving home, I walked over to the Golden Fortune Cookie and drank. Alone. And a lot.

To Mr. Wong's delight, I finally partook in his Shaolin Punch. And as advertised, it kicked my ass. After my third one, Mr. Wong could tell that I was nursing a broken heart, and he knew exactly who broke it.

Sympathetically, he approached me and said, "Remember my friend, it's like Confucius say, *If you love someone set them free… free, free, set them free…*"

"Oh for Christ sake, enough!" I snapped. "What's Confucius gonna say next? That I should send out an SOS? Or a message in a bottle? Huh? Face it, all your stupid quotes are from Sting or the Police, NOT from Confucius! Fuck!"

As Mr. Wong's bright smile faded, I immediately regretted my outburst. I'd like to blame it on the Shaolin Punch, but the truth was I was just being an asshole.

"I'm sorry, Mr. Wong. I don't mean to take things out on you. I… I just miss her."

"The girl with the pretty smile?" he knowingly asked.

I decided to join in on the Sting quotes and said, "Pretty smile, but a fortress around her heart."

This caused Mr. Wong to smile. He then put his hand on my shoulder and said, "Sometimes we build walls not to keep people out but to see who cares enough to try and knock them down."

"Sting?" I questioned.

He shook his head no.

"Confucius?" I asked.

"Nah," he said. "I heard it on the Oparah Winafrey show."

We both chuckled. I reached for my wallet, but Mr. Wong shook me off. I nodded in appreciation, and as he cleared my empty glass, he warmly said, "You touched her heart more than you know, my friend. Mr. Wong could tell."

"Thanks," I sadly smiled. "You're a good man, Mr. Wong."

"You pretty okay too, my friend."

27

"WORLD FULL OF NOTHING" – Depeche Mode

The final month at the restaurant absolutely dragged by. By the time Columbus Day weekend arrived, we all were more than ready for it to end. Especially me. I had no clue what was up next for me, but I knew I needed to get away from the beach and from the stupid memories of what could have been.

On more than one occasion, I was tempted to stop by Elise's grandmother's cottage and get her phone number in Vermont, but I didn't. I knew I had done and said everything I could. The ball was in her court. And yes, I hate when the ball is in their court. It's a very helpless feeling.

Columbus Day weekend was unusually warm that year

which meant we were extra busy on our final weekend. Labor Day marked the end of the summer, but Columbus Day marked the end of the year at the beach. Summer cottages were either boarded up or offered up as winter rentals. Ninety-five percent of the businesses at both beaches also shut down and boarded up for the year.

For the restaurant and shop workers, it's an overdue and welcomed weekend. An excited anticipation fills the air at the thought of being rid of the last of the tourists.

No more idiotic questions like, "How do we get to the lighthouse?" No more non-customers coming in looking for quarters for the meters. What do we look like, a bank? And no more stupid questions like this: "Are your lobsters Maine lobsters?" Really????

Of course, for the tourists, Columbus Day weekend marks the official end of their season in good ole Vacationland. The thought of heading back to their jobs, and homes, and suffering through another long New England winter, has most of them bitter and testy. Bottom line is they are far less excited about Columbus Day compared to us locals.

So, with the workers and the tourists on opposite ends of the happiness scale, it made for an interesting final weekend. The two most glaring things at the restaurant that weekend were:

1) We were out of a ton of menu items.

2) We were down to the bare minimum of a crew.

Both things didn't sit well with the impatient and cranky tourists.

Not only was Elise gone, but our dishwasher was back at school, and Phil took the weekend off for a family wedding in Connecticut. That just left the four Musketeers; Megan, Freddy, Todd, and myself. In other words, our final day was a huge shit-show!

I had Megan take a black marker and cross out everything on the menus that we were out of. I also instructed her and Freddy to politely point out and apologize that due to this being our last day, we were out of a lot of items.

This is how our day started: Megan's first table of the day ordered not one, not two, but three items on the crossed out list… the black marker crossed out list.

"Yeah, we're out of that too. The items crossed out in big, bold black marker means we are out of them," Megan said with more than a little sarcasm.

The following hour sounded like this:

"I'm sorry, we're closing for the season today, so we're actually out of that."

"I know this is crossed out, but do you have any fried scallops?"

"Ummm, no. That's why it's crossed out!"

There was also a lot of mumbling under the breath – from 'us' and 'them'. It didn't take long for the dining room to fill up and for the slips to start stacking up in the kitchen.

Despite Todd and I working like a finely tuned machine, even we couldn't keep up.

The dining room was even worse. Between waiting on tables and busing their own tables, Freddy and Megan were running around like chickens with their heads cut off. In Freddy's case, like a headless chicken wearing a FRANKIE SAYS RELAX tee shirt and tight powder blue shorts. So tight in fact, that when he bent over to pick something up off the floor, he ripped a giant hole in his ass.

After I provided my red-faced, hyperventilating waiter a paper bag to breath into, I then took a page out of Phil's book. Yup, Freddy's powder blue shorts were now accented with a silver duct tape ass patch. Phil would have been proud.

I made it the whole summer without bothering Mr. Murphy, so I knew calling him for backup was out of the question. But we were in desperate need of another body, so I was left with only one other option. Doug.

It had been years since Doug worked at Murphy's, but he was quick to point out, "I'm sure it's just like riding a bike."

Remind me never to watch Doug ride a bike. Actually, I'm just kidding. It wasn't bad at all. Not only did he help us out in the kitchen, but he helped bus tables in the dining room as well.

For the most part, the customers were patient and tolerable; for the most part. Of course, there's always that guy, that loud, impatient, and obnoxious guy. This one was in his mid-thirties and had a thick Boston accent. Shocking.

Upon seating him and his wife, Freddy politely informed them we were short-staffed and it might be a long wait. The dude's wife seemed understanding. The dude not so much. From that point on, he turned into a comedian. A loud comedian. A loud, obnoxious, non-funny comedian. He was the type of guy who would purposely order everything that was crossed out, and then dramatically act shocked when Freddy informed him we were out of them. With each item, he'd make a bigger scene to his 'audience'. He was also the kind of guy who actually thought people were laughing with him not at him. Dumb bastard.

His wife ordered a burger, and he finally settled on a haddock sandwich. A haddock sandwich with, "well-done fries! None of this soggy, limp fries shit," he eloquently stated.

From that point on, every time poor Freddy walked by their table, the dude had a smartass comment to make. For example:

"You do know you have duct tape on your ass, right? Not that I was checking out your ass. Though, you'd probably like that." He then turned to what he thought was his audience for approval. Uncomfortable looks were all he got.

That didn't deter him from continuing to spew his rhetoric. About ten minutes later, he waved Freddy down and loudly said, "Did they have to get on a boat and go catch the fish or what?"

To Freddy's credit, he just politely smiled and apologized again for the wait. Freddy kept coming in the kitchen, anxiously checking on the progress, but the order was still buried in our stack. I felt badly for Freddy, but we weren't going to cave in and move the dickhead's order to the front. Unfortunately, it was poor Freddy who paid the price.

At one point, the guy said to Freddy, "Hey sweetheart, if you want, I can go cook the order myself. It's not rocket science."

Freddy forced a smile and again apologized.

"You do know this will reflect in your tip," the guy said. He then followed it by laughing and saying, "I'm just kidding. I'm just busting your balls. Although, you probably like that, huh?"

At that point, the dude's wife shot him a stern look and before she could apologize on her husband's behalf, Freddy had bolted back into the kitchen and told us every detail of what was going on. Again, I should have just caved and moved their order to the front, but I didn't. Impatient pricks like that shouldn't be rewarded or catered to.

With every order that was delivered that wasn't his, he'd get louder... more obnoxious... more prickish.

The final straw came when he watched Freddy serve the table next to him.

"Are you fuckin' kidding me?" he said glaring at his wife.

Before she could tell him to calm down, he shoved a cigarette in his mouth.

Although it was still legal to smoke in restaurants back in '95, Mr. Murphy chose not to allow it. Hence the many NO SMOKING signs throughout the place. That didn't stop the obnoxious prick from lighting up anyway.

Knowing how Freddy was with confrontations, I assumed he was pissing his pants. If he wasn't, he would be in a second.

As Freddy walked by the guy's table, he grabbed Freddy's arm and angrily said, "I suggest the next time you exit the kitchen, it's with my fuckin' fish sandwich! Understand?"

Freddy informed me later, that he indeed, peed a little at that point. When he released Freddy's arm, Freddy rushed towards the kitchen. Before Freddy got far, the guy yelled out, "And bring me a fuckin' ashtray, princess!"

Freddy burst through the kitchen door, and as soon as I got him calmed down, he told us what the guy had said. The golden rule of business, especially the restaurant business, is the customer is always right. But on October 9th 1995, that rule would gloriously be broken.

Calmly, I told Todd to cook a fish sandwich. I then instructed Freddy to sit on the stool and take deep breaths. I grabbed a small plate and headed out the back door. This is where our employees who smoke go and take their breaks. I approached the ash bucket and scooped a bunch of then onto the plate then I returned to the kitchen.

When the fish sandwich was ready, I gently placed it on the plate of ashes and said, "There, one fish sandwich and one ashtray. Just as the customer ordered."

Doug and Todd cracked smiles. Freddy did not. His eyes nearly popped out of his head.

"You want me to bring this out to him like this???" Freddy said.

"Sometimes Freddy, the customer is NOT always right and they need to be shown that," I said. "Besides, I know how much you love your shenanigans."

"I... I do, but... I can't. I just can't."

"I'll fuckin' do it," said Todd.

I smiled and handed the plate to Todd. As he took it, he looked at me and hesitantly said, "Are you sure about this?"

"Fuck it," I said. "It's our last day, right? Might as well go out with a bang."

Todd's smile grew as he nodded in agreement. With the plate in hand, he headed out into the dining room. Naturally, Freddy, Doug, and I all rushed over to the door to watch the special delivery in action.

"Oh my God. Oh my God," Freddy kept nervously repeating. "I'm gonna pee my pants. Again."

Out in the dining room, Todd walked over to the dude and placed the plate in front of him and said, "Here's your fish sandwich, and here's your ashtray. It's on the house."

As Todd walked away, the man's face was bright red. It

was partly in anger but mostly in embarrassment. Especially considering everyone's eyes were on him and were snickering *at* him. You could tell he was tempted to make a giant scene, but instead, on the urging of his wife, they simply stood up and left.

When the door closed behind him, you could have heard a pin drop. And then, out of the blue, the entire restaurant burst into huge applause. Todd was greeted with high-fives from strangers and multiple hugs from Freddy.

"That must of felt phenomenal," I said.

All Todd could say was, "Mr. Murphy is gonna be so pissed."

"Nah, he's never gonna find out," I said. "It's not like we have cameras in here or anything."

"It really did feel pretty phenomenal," he smiled.

So that's how the summer of '95 officially ended at Murphy's Oceanside Restaurant.

28

"BULLETPROOF" - Radiohead

Once the *Closed For The Season* sign went up, it took a week or so to get the restaurant cleaned spotless (semi-spotless). At one point during the week, Mr. Murphy stopped in and called me into his office. What happened in that little meeting took me completely by surprise.

I knew he was happy with how I ran the place for him that summer. His spontaneous "pop-ins" where few and far between, and he admitted that he had golfed more that summer than the previous three combined. Not only did the old man show his appreciation with glowing compliments, but he handed me a big fat bonus check.

When I finally finished thanking him for the third time,

he said he had something else he wanted to talk about with me. I knew exactly what was coming next. He was going to use that moment to sweet talk me into running the place for him again next summer. I was partially right. He wanted me back, but not as the manager, but as the owner. Mr. Murphy wanted to lease the place to me. To me.

***

The following weekend, Mr. and Mrs. Murphy had a small end-of-the-year get together at their house, and as luck would have it, I was the only one without a date. Phil brought Marissa, Freddy brought Steve, Todd had his girlfriend Kerri with him, and even Megan brought her newest boy, Jason.

Most end of the year parties simply consisted of drinking, laughing, and retelling all the crazy shit that happened that summer. This party was no different. We did leave out the fish sandwich/ashtray story, however.

Mr. and Mrs. Murphy were entertained and grossed out by the Geoff/bathroom stories. They were also amused by Freddy as he recounted exactly how he and Steve met; right down to what Steve was wearing, where he was sitting, and what he ordered. Even Phil retold how he and Marissa met. It wasn't nearly as detailed as Freddy's story, but I do believe the word weedwacker was used once or thrice.

I know it sounds silly, but hearing everyone's relationship stories made me wish I had one about me and

Elise. Luckily, there was enough alcohol and laughs to take my mind off of it somewhat.

Mrs. Murphy even got into the act by telling how she and Mr. M met forty years ago. Her story took forever to tell because Mr. Murphy kept interrupting and disagreeing about her details. By 10pm, I had enough. After I said my goodbyes to Mr. and Mrs. M, I moved on to Megan.

"You outta here?" she asked.

"Yeah, I think so," I said. "Where's your new man?"

"He's in the kitchen making me another drink."

"Wow. He actually seems like a nice guy."

"You sound surprised," she smiled. "Eh, who am I kidding, I'm shocked as shit myself. He's definitely a good one. Let's hope I don't fuck it up."

"Ah yes, the whole sabotage thing, huh?"

"I'm telling ya, Josh, it's a real thing."

"Yeah, so I've seen," I said.

"I really am sorry how things turned out with Elise. For the record, I thought it was super-sweet how you put in so much effort to get to know her this summer."

"A lot of good it did me," I said.

"Trust me, Josh, it wasn't you. She just had a lot of baggage. Most of us chicks do," she said as she jokingly nudged me.

"Yeah, yeah, yeah," I smiled back. "Well, I should get going."

"Hey, do you mind if I use you as a reference? I totally

need to start looking for a winter job."

"I can do one better," I said. "I talked to Doug the other day and he said he can get you a job at the bar where he works."

"Are you kidding me? Aww, see, you really are the best!" she said giving me a big hug.

It was at that point, Phil strode over.

"You leaving, bossman?"

"That I am, Phil."

I stuck my hand out for a shake, but Phil just offered his typical salute. And speaking of saluting, Phil had joined the Marines. He'd be shipping out for boot camp two weeks later. That's right, duct tape/weedwacker Phil would be defending our country. God bless America.

"It was very interesting working with you this summer, Phil. Very, very interesting. If I don't see you before you leave, good luck and be safe."

"Yes sir, bossman," Phil said with a final salute.

He turned to walk away and I said, "Hey Phil, you do know you'll be using real guns and not potato guns, right?"

He widely smiled, "I'm counting on it."

Before I could say another word, I felt a rapid tapping on my shoulder. It was Freddy giving me one of his looks.

"You weren't going to leave without saying goodbye to moi, were you?"

"Of course not, Freddy. How could I leave without saying goodbye to my favorite dishwasher, waiter, karaoke extraordinaire?"

"Oh youuuu!" blushed Freddy. "Listen, Joshua, I really am sorry about what happened at my party. I…"

"It's okay, Freddy. It's okay."

"May I?" he asked with arms opened wide.

"You may," I laughed.

With that, he gave me a big, awkward hug and said to me, "You're a good man, Charlie Brown."

"You're a good man too, Merc," I said with a wink.

He blushed and looked at Megan. "See, I told you people call me that!"

As Freddy gloated, I made my way over to Todd and his girlfriend Kerri.

"Well, I'm outta here. It was nice to finally meet you, Kerri," I said.

"You too, Josh. Todd has talked about you all summer."

"Oh I'm sure he has," I smirked.

Kerri used that moment to excuse herself to get another drink.

"She's really nice," I said.

"Yeah," he said, "and I still have no idea what she is doing with me."

"I was thinking the same thing," I joked. "I'm just kidding, man."

After a moment of silence, Todd finally said, "Hey, I was wrong about your intentions with Elise. I still think you were trying to get into her pants," he smiled, "but I do know you were really into her and nice to her. I'm sorry things didn't work out."

"Thanks, but it is what it is."

"And I'm sorry I was such a dick all summer. You were actually a pretty good boss. Not nearly as annoying as I thought you'd be."

"Hmm, I'll take it," I said.

"It's just that over the years Mr. Murphy had a track record for hiring know-it-all, asshole managers, and I just assumed you'd be like the rest."

"Trust me, Todd, I get it. His track record for hiring useless asshole managers goes way back to when I used to work here."

"The real reason I think I was such a miserable dick was I was pissed at myself."

"For what?" I asked.

"For still being stuck working for Mr. M. Not only did Kerri graduate from college at the top of her class, but she now has a cushy job at a huge marketing company over in Portsmouth. Paid vacations, benefits; all that shit. And here I am, a college drop-out, still working at the beach in the summer."

"I totally, totally get it, Todd. Like I said before, we're a lot alike."

"Well, at least in your case you're back as a manager and not just a fuckin' cook. Not to mention, I heard Mr. M offered you to lease the place from him next year."

"Jesus! How'd you hear that?" I said. "Maybe there really are hidden cameras throughout the place."

"I'm happy for you," Todd said. "And the way my life is going, I'm sure you can pencil me in as your fuckin' cook next year."

"Yeah, I don't know about that," I said.

"Oh..." Todd said taken aback.

"I didn't mean it that way," I said. "I just meant I won't be making that decision. I turned his offer down."

"You did? Why?"

"It was quite the generous offer, and believe it or not, I actually had a lot of fun there this summer, for the most part. But... this just isn't what I want to do. Not that I know exactly what I want to do yet, but I think it'll be easier figuring that out if I'm not at the restaurant."

Still surprised, Todd just stood there and shook his head.

"What? You think I'm crazy for turning him down, huh?"

"Well, yeah, kinda," he said. "I wouldn't have turned it down, but then again, he would never make that offer to me."

"What would you say if I told you he was this close to asking you to be the manager this past summer?"

"I'd say you're crazy," laughed Todd.

"It's true. He told me himself, but he didn't think you wanted it, or was ready to be the manager," I said. "But I've watched you all summer, Todd, and you know exactly what you're doing. You know this place inside and out. And despite what you may think, you're a good team player. You might be a wiseass, but I've seen you come to the defense of everyone at work. Well, except for Chad, but fuck Chad!"

Todd laughed. "Thanks. Maybe I should apply for manager next year then," he said and laughed again. "Although, I guess that would be the call of the new owner. Hopefully Mr. M doesn't lease it out to a major dickass."

"I gave him a pretty good recommendation of someone," I said.

"Your friend, Doug," he asked.

"Doug? No way. He'd turn the Oceanside Restaurant into the Oceanside Bar. He'd probably add a stripper pole too. Not that that's a bad thing, but I'm pretty sure Mr. M wouldn't appreciate turning his life's work into that. Not to mention, I'm sure Mrs. M wouldn't appreciate it either."

"Yeah, probably not," Todd laughed.

"Mr. Murphy wants someone to take over who will keep the integrity of the place. He also wants someone who has a connection to this place. That's why I recommended you."

"Yeah, right," Todd scoffed rolling his eyes.

"I did. I might have been the manager this summer, but never once did I have to manage you. You knew exactly what needed to be done. Did you ever wonder why I always scheduled you on my days off? I knew the place would be in good hands."

Todd let my words sink in then said, "But I don't know anything about leasing a business."

"Relax, Todd. I'm sure Mr. M will take you under his wing until you get the hang of it."

I could tell Todd's mind was racing a mile a minute.

"And what about money? I don't have any money to give him up front."

"Relax. I'm sure he'll work something out with you."

Before Todd could offer more of his worrisome thoughts, Mr. Murphy walked over to us.

"I thought you were leaving?" Mr. Murphy said to me.

"I am. Just saying my goodbyes," I said.

"Did you inform Todd about our little conversation?"

"We were just talking about that," I answered.

"So, is this something you might be interested in?" he asked Todd.

"Umm… yes sir. I think I would be."

"Good. We should meet up sometime this week and get the ball rolling."

"Get the ball rolling for what?" asked Kerri rejoining the conversation.

"I might be leasing the restaurant from Mr. Murphy next summer," Todd said fighting back a smile.

"Really? Aww, honey, that's awesome." Kerri gave Todd a big hug, and I used that moment as my exit.

29

"SEASICK YET STILL DOCKED" – Morrissey

After I left the party, I ended up driving by Elise's grandmother's cottage. It was already boarded up for the winter. I parked in the driveway and thought about the last time I was there; babbling about how we should take 'us' to the next level... how we should visit each other as much as possible... how she was like a greatest hits album. Ugh!

I hate to admit it, but for the next couple of summers, I found myself making the occasional drive-by in hopes of seeing her blue Honda Accord parked here. I'm not sure what I would have done if I actually saw her car here, but sadly, I was never faced with that dilemma.

The next morning, I strangely found myself wide awake by sunrise. With all the beach stores closed, I was forced to head into the village. I grabbed a large coffee at Rick's Restaurant then headed back to the beach.

As the sun made its way into the fall sky, I sat on a bench staring out at the ocean and the beach. The same beach that six weeks earlier would have been scattered with couples taking an early morning walk. But now, on the edge of November, besides the occasional person letting their dog run free on the beach, there was no one. Just the sounds of seagulls and the waves.

It's kind of ironic, we spend the whole summer bitchin' and moaning about the tourists, but when we finally get *our* beach back, it's a little bittersweet, especially when the summer ended less than expected.

As I sat there, I sipped my coffee and took a deep breath. It was as if I could still smell the summer; fried dough, the Goldenrod's taffy, and a heavy dose of tropical suntan lotions.

I leaned back on the bench and closed my eyes. I saw the chaos of the restaurant, the parties, the bars, the lazy beach days, the basketball games, the runaway ball trick, the late night walkabouts, and even the sounds of various video games from the Fun-O-Rama. It was as if the ghosts of summers past were haunting and echoing in my mind.

I also couldn't help replaying certain songs in my head;

certain 'summer songs' that would be forever linked to the sights and sounds of summers past. But when I finally opened my eyes, however, all I was left with was an empty beach. An empty, quiet beach.

The End... for now

ABOUT THE AUTHOR

JODY CLARK

Jody grew up in the Kittery/York area of southern Maine. He originally started out as a screenwriter. As of now, he has written nine feature-length screenplays ranging from dramas to dramedies to comedies. Not only did Jody grow up in Maine, but he makes it a point to utilize and represent his state as much as possible. From Maine's scenic rocky coast, to its remotely pristine backwoods, to its eclectic characters; all serve as backdrops and pay homage to his beloved state. His ultimate goal is not to just sell his scripts, but to have them filmed right here in the great state of Maine.

Unfortunately, searching for the proper financing has been a long, tiring, and at times, disheartening process. Feeling helpless in the whole 'funding' process, Jody decided to reverse the typical Hollywood blueprint. That blueprint being: It's almost ALWAYS a novel that gets turned into a screenplay and not a screenplay which gets turned into a novel. Jody's thought process was simple: It's much easier to self-publish a book rather than self-finance a movie, and who knows, maybe, just maybe, this will be a screenplay that gets turned into a book only to eventually get turned back into a movie! But even if this wild idea never comes to fruition, at least by turning it into a novel, the *stories* themselves will be able to be enjoyed by the public. Whether it's two or two million people who buy his books, Jody is just happy that they are no longer collecting dust in a desk drawer.

VACATIONLAND

BOOKS

THE WAY BOOKS SHOULD BE.
STORIES SET IN MAINE
BY PEOPLE WHO LIVE THERE

Vacationlandbooks.com

Jody Clark